GW00760013

1

Amy Tierney still lives in Wicklow, with her husband, three children and two dogs. The family have recently adopted a goldfish called Ben.

April... is the second book in the "Calendar Days Series".

Amy Tierney

April...

Email: <u>Amie.Tierney@hotmail.com</u>

Text ©copyright Amy Tierney 2017

All rights reserved. No part of this publication may be reproduced or utilised in any form or by any means, electronic or mechanical, including photocopying, recording or in any information storage or retrieval system, without permission in writing from the publisher or Author.

Edited by Eamon O'Cleirigh

Clearview Fiction Editing

ISBN-13: 978-1543219562

For my Mam and Dad

X

1st April 2014

Tuesday

A hand inched its way up Cathy's leg, its fingers caressing the inside of her thigh. A gentle moan spilled out of her parched mouth as a touch so soft brushed over her skin. Hot breath brought goose bumps as lips kissed the pulse in her neck. Exquisite sensations spread through her body, slick with arousal, throbbing and twisting in the hope he would soon put her out of her misery and bring her to a crashing climax. Only then would she return the sensual favour.

Her eyes flew open, and she looked around the darkened room in confusion. Disappointment flushed through her as she realised she was alone. She'd been dreaming. *Feck!* Vivid images of Sam danced through her mind, pulling her too fast into the waking world.

Even though it had only been two nights since she'd experienced the feelings for real, Cathy couldn't dismiss the aches gnawing at her. She wanted Sam O'Keefe in her bed, now, satisfying her needs with every touch.

Each time he visited, she went from a total high when he arrived, to hitting rock bottom when he had to leave again. She knew this was because of her insistence they keep the relationship going after Sam had moved to London, and she battled every day with the jumble of emotions brought up by dealing with a long-distance relationship. Things were tough, they both knew that, but their love for each other held the pieces together, despite the hurdles that popped up along the way.

She checked the bedside clock, which blinked a steady six-thirty back at her. Just for once, she wished she could hit the pause button on the day, stay in bed, and wallow in a well-deserved bout of self-pity. But this was real life, and real-life Cathy had six-year-old twins already making a racket in the other bedroom.

As if on cue, the floorboards thumped as the children made their way towards her bedroom. She couldn't help but laugh when one twin, while trying to cover their giggles, farted, sending them both into hysterics.

They got their act together and burst into her bedroom.

"Mammy, Mammy, save us," Millie squealed.

"Save us, quick, save us," Jack cried.

"Hey, hey, you two, calm down. What's wrong?"

"We saw a mouse," Millie said, waving her arms around like a windmill, while Jack did a little dance beside her that showed how he'd leapt out of the rodent's way.

"It wasn't a mouse," he said. "No, it was a rat!"

Cathy kneeled up on the bed, wide awake now, clutching the duvet to her chest. "Oh, sweet Jesus," she screeched, causing the children to topple off the bed, half in fright, half through laughter. "Where?"

Panic swept through her. *A bloody mouse in the house!* This was the last thing she needed. Spiders, she could just about handle, but a rodent? No way, that was definitely a deal-breaker. They would have to move – a method of escape against the infestation was already forming in her brain.

"Tell me exactly where you saw it," she ordered, failing miserably at being brave in front of the kids. Her gaze darted across the floor, checking the doorway. She crouched, ready to spring up at a moment's notice.

When she looked over at her children, she noticed how calm they were, and wondered if they'd concussed themselves falling off the bed. Millie and Jack stood side by side, hand in hand, a broad grin across both of their faces.

"April Food's day, Mammy," they shouted, doubling over with laughter at their own joke.

Cathy's relief took her breath away. She grabbed the twins and squeezed them with sheer delight. "You little monkeys," she said, failing to sound stern. "You nearly gave me a heart attack."

"It was a good April Food's joke, wasn't it, Mammy?" Jack asked. "We got you."

"Yes, you got me," she said, her heart taking on a more regular beat, "but it's called April Fools, not April Foods." She tickled them into submission, making them promise they would never trick her with talk of mice, or rats, or any other four-legged creatures running around their house again.

The three of them settled down, cuddling in together. Cathy stroked two silky blonde heads, relishing five more minutes of snuggles before they had to get up and press play on the day ahead.

***

Cathy dropped the children off at school, reminding them that their dad would be picking them up later.

"Don't forget to ring me to say good-night," she said, kissing each of them, before sending them on their way into the senior-infants' classroom.

"Bye, Mam," they called as they raced through the door, away for yet another night. She'd miss them, as always, but they loved spending time with their father. *Gary had better not be late collecting them.*

On the way home, she checked her phone, looking for any contact from Sam. She couldn't shake the feelings churned up by the dream this morning, leaving her turned on and hot, desperate to hear his voice again. The phone remained silent.

With the car parked in her driveway, she looked for any new emails, groaning when she spotted one that made her heart sink.

Loulou@hotmail.com glared back at her off the screen.

"Damn," she muttered, running a hand through her tangled hair. She didn't have the energy to face this one today. This woman, Lou Lou Fleming, was becoming a major pain in the ass. Email after email, phone calls, texts, voice mails – even a note taped to her front door on one occasion. *This woman is out of control.* She unlocked her front door and went inside.

"Will I? Won't I?" she said out loud, trying to decide if opening the email was a wise decision.

"Feck it. May as well get it over with." She took a deep breath and opened the message with a tap of the screen.

From: Loulou@hotmail.com

To: Byron Kelly, Cathy Byrne, Annabel Clancy, Sally Coffey, Natasha De Luca, Nicola Carr, Linda Coleman, Michelle Devlin, Sarah Doyle, Janet Glynn, Annmarie Kearney, Helen Kearney, Brenda O'Brien.

Subject: Final arrangements for Hen weekend.

Hi Girls,

Are we all excited about this weekend's major celebrations? It's finally here............ BYRON'S HEN PARTY EXTRAVAGANZA.

I've attached a detailed document of all the activities organised, as well as the schedule. You will all be expected to follow this format, if we want this weekend to be perfect for our blushing bride to be.

Please note, there has been a change of plan for the group-costume idea. I need you to all be on board 100% with this new theme. It's all or nothing, girls. If one person drops the ball, it will ruin the effect we are trying to achieve. I don't have time to change this all again, girls, so please, no moaning. Details of what is needed are on the attached file, so put up or shut up (yes, that is directed at you, Annabel Clancy. No bitchy remarks this time, please).

Today, I need you all to reply ASAP with confirmation of who is rooming with who at the hotel. I have five double rooms and two triples, so figure it out between yourselves.

Let me know who is with who, and I can update my spreadsheet.

That's it for now. With only four days to go, the excitement is mighty. I bet you all can't wait to party, party, party, girls.

If I have any further ideas, or changes to the schedule, I will let you all know.

Bye for now,

Lou Lou x x

      "Jesus," Cathy said, shaking her head. She was almost afraid to open the file attachment, dreading the torture that awaited them. Biting the bullet, she clicked on the icon.

She had to sit, overwhelmed by the sheer volume of information flooding onto the small screen.

This is like a military operation, and the sergeant major has spoken. She rolled her eyes.

She scrolled through the attachment, trying to figure out how on earth Lou Lou had come up with all this stuff. Travel details to Kilkenny City were timed to the nearest minute – including two ten-minute stops along the route in case of bathroom emergencies. Bags of accessories, needed for the weekend's antics, would be evenly distributed between cars; each driver was issued with a number indicating the position of their car in the convoy traveling down the N7 motorway – no deviations permitted. And costumes – all attendees, with the exception of the bride, were required to wear a black, knee-length dress, nude tights, and black heels. Byron was to wear red. *Accessories* were being provided by Lou Lou, but were being kept top secret until they all arrived in Kilkenny.

"Oh, God," she said, "that could be anything."

A hair and make-up session was arranged for four o'clock at the hotel. No excuses or exceptions made. Everyone must attend. Lou Lou stressed that their look as a group must be uniformed, and this included hairstyles and make-up. Red nail varnish was preferred – you could choose your own shade.

She'd scheduled pre-dinner drinks for seven that evening, followed by a short taxi ride to the town centre. Dinner would be in Langton's at eight-thirty and it was imperative they not be late.

13

A fleet of town cars would be on standby, prepared to arrive at a moment's notice on Lou Lou's command to provide transport from venue to venue for the whole evening, ensuring they all stayed together and stood out as the hen party to be reckoned with.

Pre-paid tickets to the nightclub would be distributed after dinner.

Cathy shuddered as she read the instructions again. *Jesus Christ, this is going to cost me a fortune.* The money she would spend this weekend would feed herself and the children for a fortnight. But on the other hand, Byron Kelly was her best friend, and she would never let her down.

No doubt there would be plenty of *L* signs pinned to a pink bride-to-be sash, and inflatable willies at every turn, but she couldn't help but cringe at the expense of all the frivolous extras. The last few months had seen her saving hard, knowing this hen party was something she couldn't miss. She was one of the bridesmaids, for Christ's sake – she had to be there. It was just, as a single mother of two children, she could think of better ways to spend the little bit of money she had.

Her phone rang, and not surprisingly, Byron's name flashed up.

"Is that Lou Lou one on the same planet as the rest of us?" Byron asked, the same frustration evident in her voice as Cathy was experiencing. "Did you get the email, Cathy? Did you read the attachment? Dear God, what am I going to do?"

"Well," Cathy said, smiling as she flicked a speckle of fluff off her knee, "you did make your new best friend, Lou Lou Fleming, head of the party committee."

"Oh, shut up, you. Stop being so smug." Bryon groaned. "You know I was backed into a corner on this one. When she heard I'd nothing special planned, she took over and organised the whole thing."

Cathy bit back an audible chuckle at her friend's distress. "You could have stopped her."

"I couldn't," Byron whined. "Her mother isn't long dead and I felt sorry for her. She needed something to take her mind off things and, well, you know…this just happened to come along. Perfect timing, eh?"

Cathy laughed. "Yeah, perfect for her."

"And, anyway, how was I to know she would organise the party like a bloody military operation going into battle?"

"Well, my friend, according to the introduction email she sent us a few weeks ago, she is, and I quote – 'the top project manager in your company, with a one-hundred percent success rate in providing first-class services to all her clients, while managing the internal and external needs of the company'. She says it herself – she's the best."

"Stop laughing, Cathy. What am I going to do? It's going to be a bloody nightmare. Everyone's texting me, giving out about her. All the rules and instructions! It's not right to be asking people to do all that. We're supposed to be going away to relax – let our hair down. Instead, she has an appointment made for four on Saturday to go and get it put up again. Jesus, give me strength."

Cathy couldn't help but laugh again at the panic in her friend's voice.

"Hold on, Cathy, wait until I read you out the text I got this morning." She cleared her throat. "Sarah wants to know if there's any time scheduled in for hooking up with a fella and getting a bit of action while she's there."

"Eww, dirty stop-out." Cathy hooked her feet under her legs, picturing Sarah throwing a punch in Lou Lou's direction if she didn't get the chance to score.

"Michelle and Natasha are sharing with Lou Lou. They've come up with a plan to pour tequila down her neck before they leave the room – try to loosen her up at bit. Oh, God, I can see this all going terribly wrong."

"Just relax, Byron. It'll be grand. So what if the sergeant major has written a rule book on behaviour for the weekend? Most of the girls going on this trip won't give a crap about sticking to a schedule, or following a list. They'll do their own thing. You need to relax and enjoy yourself. Forget about Lou Lou. Just go with the flow." Cathy worked a finger through a tangle in her hair. "Look, don't worry, if it gets too much, we'll ditch the crazy bitch in Langton's and go to Matt the Millers instead."

"Ah, I know all that, Cathy. It's just nerves, I guess. It's not often we get to go away together, and I don't want people forced to do stuff they don't want to do. They should be able to relax and enjoy themselves."

"We will," Cathy said, keeping a gentle tone in her voice. "One way or another, this group of girls will have Kilkenny painted a bright red come Sunday morning. Don't you worry about it, we'll have a blast."

Full of divilment, she brought up a subject she knew would freak Byron out. "You know this is only the start of the worry and stress?" She kept her voice all innocent. "It will be much, much worse for you when Tom goes on his stag weekend."

There followed an expected silence. Then, "I told you before, Tom is not having a stag weekend. He doesn't believe in such traditions. He would much prefer a quiet night in with his friends, having a few beers and playing cards."

Cathy snorted at the barefaced lie. "Oh, yes, and pigs are circling the airport, waiting for landing instruction from the control tower. Pull the other one, ya mad egg."

"Shut up, you," Byron snapped. "It's not funny. I don't want to even think about all that. Oh, shit, I have to go. Lou Lou's making a beeline for my desk, carrying an armful of black feathery boas. Oh,

17

Jesus, what the…? Oh, hi, Lou Lou. Erm…just hold on a sec and I'll finish my call to a client." Byron's cough was backed by a low groan. "Hello? Can I get back to you a little later on that deal? Thank you so much for your support."

The phone went dead and Cathy chuckled and shook her head at the thought of poor Byron trying to keep a straight face while Lou Lou explained what the feather boas were for. If she wasn't careful, Byron would tell Lou Lou where she could stick the boa – no mistake. And though she was kind of sorry for what her best friend was going through, with the Henzilla intent on organizing her life away, it was all a bit of craic, and went a long way to lightening the mood. She scanned through the list of instructions again, checking for what she needed to do in preparation for the weekend ahead.

2nd April

Wednesday

Sam's mind wandered as he stood in line, waiting for his coffee. Images of Cathy, two nights before, flooded his mind. He shifted to relieve his stiffening cock, buttoning his coat to hide the obvious signs of arousal in his trousers.

This is worse than being a teenager. He grabbed his coffee and made a quick exit, out into the freedom of anonymity.

A couple of minutes later, he dodged his way through the crowded tube platform, searching for a suitable spot where he could stop and wait for the next train. Commuting in London was a drag, but even though he could afford to travel by taxi or car, he found public transport more reliable than getting stuck in the city gridlock every day.

Once the train arrived, he squeezed his way on, lucky to locate a pole to grab on to and settle in for the thirty-minute journey out of town.

Sorcha had called him last night, eager to chat. She'd issued a rare invitation to meet up after school, something he took as a positive sign that things were starting to move in the right direction, considering he'd initiated all meetings in the past. As always, today's meeting would be chaperoned by Aoife, her adopted mother.

Despite the icy exterior his daughter held up, he believed it was beginning to thaw, at last. Even at the tender age of ten, Sorcha knew her own mind. She only did the things she wanted to do, and always at her own pace. Even though it pained him, he'd let her take the reins for the past six months, watching and waiting for a sign that she was willing to accept him into her life. This might be just the breakthrough he was waiting for.

As people exited at the next stop, Sam found an empty seat and relaxed back into the journey. He sipped his coffee and shuddered, remembering the disaster the first few months in London had turned out to be. The shock of finding out about Sorcha's existence, coupled with the pain of having to leave Cathy, had left him feeling like he'd been torn in two.

Aoife and Bill, Sorcha's parents, wouldn't let him anywhere near her when he'd first made contact. Weeks of pleading and begging fell on deaf ears until, as a last resort, he'd threatened legal action. He threw all sorts of stupid money at lawyers, instructing them to fight tooth and nail, if necessary. All he wanted was access to the daughter that, until recently, he hadn't known about.

Now, as he looked out the window at the passing countryside, he shook his head in disbelief. *Dickhead. Who the hell did I think I was?*

He'd finally calmed and tried the softly-softly approach his lawyers had suggested. They contacted Aoife and Bill on his behalf, explaining the difficult situation Sam now found himself in. All he wanted was to meet his daughter.

Weeks passed again before a breakthrough arrived. Aoife and Bill had been in contact with Sinead, Sorcha's birth mother, after which they agreed to let him meet Sorcha for the first time. The date, December 15th, would forever be engrained in his mind. Despite shyness from Sorcha, nervousness from her parents, and a touch of hyperactivity from him, he would never forget their first meeting. That was the first chip he'd seen falling from the iceberg, and it had continued to melt, bit by bit, ever since.

As the train pulled into the station, fresh nerves surged through him. *Will these butterflies ever go away?* Each time they met, he got to know her a little bit more. He was in no doubt she was controlling the relationship, but that was okay for now – the time would come when it felt right for both of them to continue on with their lives, either as close relatives, or maybe with him looking on from afar. Time would determine the outcome, but for now, he was happy to visit and talk and get to know his daughter.

He walked the short distance from the train station to the shopping centre where they had arranged to meet. The last thing he wanted was to be late, and he checked his watch, but he needn't have worried, spotting Sorcha and Aoife strolling towards the meeting point. He quickened his step and waved, greeting them both.

"How're things?" he called out. "How's school?" He smiled at the girl, picking up on the strained atmosphere between mother and daughter.

21

What's going on here? He shook Aoife's hand, her touch clammy.

"Alright," Sorcha said, flicking her long brown hair over her shoulder and rolling her mascara-lashed eyes.

A look at Aoife yielded no clue as to what was going on, so he tried again. "I was delighted to hear from you last night." He realised he was bouncing on his toes, like a child about to get out to play, so he diverted their attention with a cough into his hand. "We, ah…haven't had a chance to catch up since I got back from Ireland."

"Yeah, too bad," Sorcha said, with another roll of her eyes.

Sam looked from her to Aoife, then back again. *What the heck is going on here?* This was one of those times he'd need to tread careful. "Is everything okay?"

"Yeah," she said again, chewing her lip and looking away.

Aoife grunted and shook her head. "Snap out of it, Sorcha. Stop being so rude." She looked at Sam, a hard frown creasing her brow. "She's been like this all week. I don't know what's got into her lately."

"Well, it's because I can't have those new trainers that I wanted so much."

"I can't afford them, Sorcha. Not this week, anyway."

Sorcha folded her arms across her chest. "It's not fair, everyone else has them."

"Well, that's great for everyone else, but you don't. Not this week, right?"

Sam saw this developing into a screaming match. He edged between them both. "Hang on a second, Sorcha. It's not fair to blame your mother if she can't afford to buy you expensive shoes at the drop of a hat. Money doesn't grow on trees, you know."

"Pfft, you sound just like Mum now. And how can you even say that? You're rich. You could buy me the trainers if you really wanted to."

"Sorcha!" Aoife snapped, embarrassment written all over her face at her daughter's audacity. "Don't speak to Sam like that. What he does with his money is none of our business. He doesn't have to buy you things, and he certainly should not be made feel guilty that you don't have something that you really want. That is not the way things work around here."

Sam grimaced inside as Aoife's guilt-laden words hit home. She was right, he didn't have to buy Sorcha things, but that didn't mean he shouldn't. How wrong could it be to treat his daughter to a gift every now and again, especially if it was something she really wanted? Unsure of where the boundaries lay, he wondered if it would solve a problem or cause more friction if he offered to buy the trainers himself.

He looked at Aoife, trying to gauge whether he would be doing the right thing. *How bad could it be, treating her to something she actually needs?* He caught her eye and nodded to the side, gesturing for her to join him.

He told her, if she didn't mind, he'd be happy to buy the trainers for Sorcha. "I don't want to step on any toes, here. I know you and Bill aren't in a great place, moneywise, so I'd like to help out, if that's all right with you."

"Sam." Aoife glanced at him, then looked down and took a deep breath. "You don't have to do that. The trainers are expensive, and Sorcha has to learn that she can't always get what she wants."

"I understand that. Look, how about this? I'll buy Sorcha the trainers—" He held up a hand as Aoife started to protest. "But only if she promises to help you out around the house for the next two weeks. We can say it's an advance on her wages, and she must do the ironing, or the washing, or whatever. If she doesn't do the work, you can take them back."

Aoife frowned again and looked away, obviously giving his suggestion serious consideration. She glanced over his shoulder several times at Sorcha, who Sam knew was continuing her stroppy sulk.

"Okay, Sam, but only if she promises to work for them."

They walked over to where Sorcha was now window-shopping at a designer-handbag shop. Her sullen face returned as Sam and Aoife approached.

"Sam has some news for you," Aoife said, waving him forward to broker the deal.

"Your mum and I have agreed that I'll buy you the trainers." He watched her expression morph from grumpy goat to fairy princess in the blink of an eye. "But, you have to promise to do everything your mum asks for the next two weeks. Hoover the floor, empty the dishwasher, even clean the bath, whatever she needs doing, you have to agree."

Sorcha squinted at her mother. "Clean the bath?" She looked up at Sam, then back to her mother. "I'm not sure the trainers are worth that—"

"Sorcha!" Aoife's warning was swift and sharp.

The young girl brightened in a flash, throwing on her doting-daughter persona. With a smile as sweet as sugar, she'd won her mother over. "I'm only joking, Mum. Of course I'll do the chores around the house. I'll do whatever you want. It's only fair, I suppose. Thank you, Sam. You're very cool." She linked her mother's arm. "We both thank you."

Sam smiled, but now wasn't sure he'd made the right move. As he followed Sorcha and Aoife towards the sports shop, he didn't like the feeling of dread washing over him, knowing he'd potentially opened up a massive can of worms.

And to make it worse, he caught the thumbs-up gesture between mother and daughter in their shop-window reflection. It reminded him of something Sinead would do. He took a deep breath and let out a quiet sigh. *What have I done?*

3rd April

Thursday

Cathy wasn't feeling great. A horrible strain of the vomiting bug was running rampant through the kids' school. The nausea hit her in waves, forcing her to stop what she was doing and put her head between her knees. She waited for it to pass, praying it didn't start flying out the other end.

Sitting on her bed, surrounded by all sorts of lotions and waxing strips, she was in no mood to preen herself. "I'll do it tomorrow," she said, grabbing the phone to dial Annabel's number.

"Hey, Annie. Are you all set for the weekend ahead?"

"Yes, just packing my little black dress and a wooden stake, in case I need to use it on Lou Lou Fleming. What are you up to?"

"I'm just sitting here trying to get motivated enough to shave my legs and pluck my eyebrows. I'm so tired, though, I just want to go to bed."

"Well, that's what you get for burning the candle at both ends with Sam. You're not twenty-five anymore, Cathy. You can't expect to have marathon sex sessions with a gorgeous hunk all weekend and not pay the price later on."

"Stop it." Cathy couldn't help but laugh. "You'll know all about marathon sex sessions as soon as Jean Luc gets back from his trip. I bet that French fella has a few pages from the Karma Sutra tucked up his sleeve."

"He knows his stuff, I'll give him that," Annabel said, "but this girl will never kiss and tell."

They chatted for a while longer, before Cathy had to apologise and run to the bathroom.

"Hello? Hello? Cathy, are you okay?"

"Sorry, Annie, just…" She gagged as bile, all that was left in her stomach, spurted out her mouth and nose.

"Jesus, Cathy, what the hell's going on there?'

"Sorry about that Annie." She grabbed tissues with her free hand. "I've, ah, got some sort of stomach flu or something. Puking all day. But I think that's the last of it now. Fingers crossed, eh?"

Silence ensued, which Cathy took advantage of to wipe her nose and mouth.

"Cathy?" Another moment's silence while Cathy wiped the toilet-bowl rim. "Don't you dare ditch me this weekend, Cathy Byrne. I don't care how sick you are, you're coming to Kilkenny with me tomorrow. No excuses."

"I can't help it if I'm sick, Annabel. I'm not doing it on purpose."

"I don't care if you have Avian Influenza, you are not leaving me alone with all those clucking hens."

"Ah, very good, Annabel, you made a joke. Bird flu, clucking hens. Get it? No? Never mind. Look, don't worry, I'm still going. I didn't spend all this money on dresses and tights and waxing strips to waste it all sitting around here feeling sorry for myself. Mum is collecting the children from school tomorrow, so I'll be ready to go at lunchtime, if that suits?"

"All right, but don't forget we're sharing a room, so we need to set a few ground rules. Number one: No men allowed in the room after eight o'clock. Number two: Door will be shut and locked at eleven sharp, no exceptions. Number three: Snoring must be kept to a minimum – there will be earplugs available upon request. Number four: Under no circumstances are you to have fun on this weekend away. We wouldn't want to upset the bride-to-be, would we?"

Cathy chuckled, feeling better as she listened to her friend take the piss out of Lou Lou Fleming.

"Nothing better than a rod up your arse and the sergeant-major approach to get a party started, don't you think?" She hoped this illness had passed by tomorrow and she could enjoy herself.

A big yawn caught her off guard. "Oh, God, Annie, that's me. This thing has me wrecked. I'll see you tomorrow. I'll meet you in town at lunchtime."

"Goodnight, sleep tight, and don't forget to bring barf bags with you tomorrow. I don't want you puking all over my car. Bird flu is not an excuse," she said, laughing as she hung up.

Cathy swept the bits and pieces off the bed and crawled under the duvet, praying for a good night's sleep and a healthier start to the morning. She'd need all her strength for whatever Lou Lou Fleming had in mind for them.

4th April

Friday

Miles of traffic stretched out in front of them as Cathy and Annabel settled in for the long journey ahead.

"Whose idea was it to leave during the middle of rush hour?" Annabel asked, her knuckles white on the steering wheel as they crept along.

"Lou Lou Fleming's," Cathy answered, changing the cd to a 1990's pop mix.

"This road is always chock-a-block. Don't you think she should've factored that into her equations?"

"You can't blame her for everything," Cathy said. "It didn't suit everyone to leave earlier, so we just have to put up with it."

"Well, if we'd been allowed to drive any route we liked, instead of in this ridiculous convoy, you and I could be there by now."

Cathy watched her friend's temper flare. Poor Annabel, she hated traffic, and being told what to do, especially from someone she saw as a stuck-up little tyrant, intent on taking the fun out of everything.

"What number car are we, anyway?" she asked, checking in front and behind.

"Number two. Bridesmaids. We're following car number one, the bride-to-be, travelling with Henzilla."

Enjoying the banter, Cathy picked up where Annabel left off. "Behind us is car number three, close friends of the bride, followed by car number four, close friends of the groom."

Annabel shifted gear. "And down the back in cars five, six, and seven, are the hanger-on hens. It doesn't matter if they get lost along the way."

"Annabel!" Cathy nearly choked on a boiled sweet. "Don't let them hear you saying that."

Annabel shrugged. "I'm only repeating what was said earlier, when Lou Lou was giving us our flight formations."

Cathy couldn't help smiling. "Is she right in the head, do you think?"

"I don't know, but one thing's for sure, this is going to be the most organised piss-up I've ever been on."

They buzzed down their windows and turned up the volume, singing along to favourite pop songs from their youth.

"You can't beat a bit of 90's cheesy pop," Cathy roared over the beat blaring from the speakers.

Once they left the city gridlock and the road opened up, Annabel put her foot down, overtaking the leading car.

"What are you doing?" Cathy shouted above the music. "Lou Lou will go mental."

Annabel waved like the queen as they passed Lou Lou's car, with Cathy trying to keep a straight face.

The music cut off as the car phone rang. Annabel answered it on Bluetooth.

"You're breaking formation, Annabel," Lou Lou said, her stern voice filling the car.

"Sorry, Lou Lou, my foot slipped," Annabel replied, biting her lip to stifle her laugh.

"Okay, well, get back into—"

"Sorry, Lou, can't hear you. You're break— This is a very b— Hello? Hello?" She gave a silent *ha, ha* to Cathy. "You're breaking— I'm going— a tunnel, and I have to—" She hit the disconnect button, licked a finger, and held it in the air, speeding away from the cars behind. "Annabel Clancy, one, Lou Lou bloody Fleming, nil."

Cathy looked back through the rear window and watched Lou Lou turn purple, while Byron gestured frantically for the other woman to calm down.

"Oh, poor Byron looks like she's getting an earful from the master manipulator. Lou Lou looks like she's ready to kill."

"It's her own fault, Cathy. She let that controlling bitch take over everything, making us all miserable. In my defence, I'm actually doing Byron a favour. I have plans to kidnap her at the first rest stop which, according to my extremely detailed travel itinerary, should be coming up very soon."

"Don't even think about it, Annabel," Cathy said, hoping her friend was only joking. "You're in enough trouble as it is. And look, can you not see that Lou Lou's intentions are good? She's worked really hard organising this weekend. So what if she's a bit controlling. Once we reach the hotel, we can ignore her and do our own thing."

"All right, but I'll be springing Byron from her deadly clutches as soon as I can. The bride-to-be deserves a great send off. She's put her heart and soul into this wedding for months now. She needs to let her hair down, not lose it through stress."

"Okay, I'll have a chat with Lou Lou when we stop," Cathy said, glancing back again. "I'll try to get her to loosen up a bit. Maybe we can swap cars, eh? You take Byron and I'll go with her. I'll talk sense into her before we reach Kilkenny."

"Okay, that might work, but, Cathy, keep her away from me. I've had my fill of that woman to last me a lifetime. Any more and I might have to kill her."

"Good, and anyway, I could do with changing cars." Cathy scrunched up her face. "Your…perfume is making me sick."

***

"Jesus, I thought she was going to crash the car," Byron said later that evening as they sat down to a quiet meal in the hotel bar. Lou Lou was off organising something, and Bryon had used the opportunity to have a few words alone with Annabel and Cathy.

Annabel smirked and raised her glass. "Got this party livened up a bit, though, didn't I?" She chuckled and sipped on her vodka tonic.

"She's not so bad, Annie, when you get to know her," Cathy said. "I had a good chat with her on the way down, explained a few things. She really adores you, Byron, and wants this whole weekend to be perfect, right down to the last edible G-string."

Byron's jaw dropped. "No way, not a hope in hell." She pushed the remains of her fish and chips away. "You can forget all about the tacky hen-party props. I am not traipsing through this town tomorrow with a rubber willy stuck to my head, or flashing boobs hanging off me."

Well, I don't know," Cathy said, giggling, "I think you'll look great in fishnet stockings, and a *Hens Go Wild* sash pinned to your dress. I had a peek earlier at the accessories Lou Lou left in the car. There is definitely some blowing to be done tomorrow night."

Annabel nearly choked on her vodka when Byron's head whipped around to stare at Cathy.

"What?" Byron said. "Are you joking? Please tell me you are joking."

Cathy shrugged. "There were quite a few inflatable penises in the bag. One for everyone in the audience, I'd say."

"Oh, crap!" Bryon closed her eyes at the sound of Lou Lou Fleming's vocal approach to their table.

"Well, girls, are we all having a nice evening?" she asked, smiling at Cathy, while ignoring Annabel.

Byron coughed and shifted in her seat. "Yes, but, Lou Lou, I'm just wondering what you have planned for tomorrow night. I don't want anything tacky. No strippers, no embarrassing memorabilia. Nothing that's going to make me gag, right?"

Lou Lou placed a hand on Byron's arm. "Don't be worrying about all that, Byron. Your only job this weekend is to relax and enjoy yourself. And look, if we use a few little extra props along the way, what harm is it? This is a hen party."

Silenced into submission, Byron just nodded and gulped down half her drink.

"Looks like you have a bit of waxing of your own to do, my friend." Annabel wiggled her eyebrows as Lou Lou walked away to torment some of the less-important guests.

5th April

Saturday

The day started well. Cathy enjoyed a luxury breakfast with Byron and Annabel, before heading out for a leisurely walk in the hotel's luscious gardens. When the rain started to fall, she decided to take advantage of the indoor leisure facilities she'd seen on their arrival.

She swam lengths in the aqua-blue pool, gliding through the cool water. As she turned at one end, she spotted a few of the girls from their group relaxing in the hot tub, sipping cocktails.

"It's a bit early for all that, don't you think?" Lou Lou Fleming swam up beside her, nodding over to the where Michelle, Sally, Sarah, and Jan were enjoying themselves.

Cathy tread the water, not wanting to be rude by turning away. "Ah, they're just enjoying themselves, Lou Lou," She smiled at the other woman. "They're doing no harm."

Lou Lou sniffed. "Well, as long as they turn up to the hair and make-up sessions I've organised at four o'clock, I suppose it's all right." She ducked under the water, turning to swim off in the opposite direction.

Rowdy goofs echoed around the hollow shell of the pool enclosure, the high ceiling amplifying every scream and squeal. Cathy waved, acknowledging the girls, eager to let them know she had no problem with their boisterous behaviour.

"Get over here, and join us," Jan shouted. "The water's only gorgeous."

"Yeah," Sally roared, "these bubbles are tickling me in places only a man can reach."

An elderly gentleman, swimming the backstroke, almost went under when he mistimed his stroke and crashed into the wall.

"Oh, sorry about that, Mister," Michelle called, standing up to check if the man was okay. Two large breasts, barely covered by tiny scraps of hot-pink material, bounced as she jumped up and down to see if old Father Time was still alive.

Cathy swam over and helped the man out of the pool, before those twenty-something-year-old floozies gave the poor guy a coronary. Barely able to contain her laughter, she pointed the man in the direction of the communal dressing room, then went to join the girls in the tub.

"Will I go and check on him?" Sarah asked, emerging out of the water in an even skimpier bikini than her friend.

Cathy put a hand on her shoulder and guided her back into the tub. "I think he'll be okay," she said, smiling at the girl's concern, not too sure the poor old devil would survive a visit from any of them.

When she stepped into the tub, she groaned with pleasure as warm bubbles massaged her feet.

This is exactly what I need. She sank into the water, letting the tub's sprays and jets work their magic on each tight muscle.

"Will you have a drink?" Sally asked, holding out a cocktail menu.

"No, I don't think so," Cathy replied, pretty sure Sally had pinched the menu from the bar. "My stomach's not the best today. I think I'll save the alcohol for later."

"Fair enough," Sally said, scanning the laminated menu herself, "I'm only drinking them now to stop last night's hangover from kicking in."

Jan raised her glass in agreement. "Hair of the dog, and all that."

Cathy loved the easy-going nature of Byron's work friends. Even though she'd met them all before, she'd never really spoken with them. Now she was enjoying their company and could see why they all got on so well. They were lovely girls. A little garish, maybe, but underneath the make-up and false nails, they were nice people.

"Where did you all end up last night?" she asked.

"Did a bit of a crawl around the town first, then on to Langton's," Sally answered. "Scored a lovely shift down in Matt the Millers."

"Oh, yeah," Jan agreed. "He was a beast. I'd say they'll be great craic tonight."

Cathy looked from one girl to the next. "Tonight?"

"We arranged to meet up with his crowd later on in the nightclub," Michelle explained. "Might even get myself a lick of someone's lolly." The small group burst into roars of laughter, the sound echoing around the pool.

Cathy just shook her head and smiled. She was by no means an innocent virgin, but she couldn't believe how much things had changed since she'd been single. In fairness, she had been pregnant on the twins at nineteen, and married at twenty-two, but still, she hadn't realised how forward young single girls were nowadays. Not a bother talking about sex, or positions – each girl getting exactly what they wanted.

Now that she was with Sam, maybe she could be a little more adventurous when it came to pleasuring herself and her man. Sex toys and accessories were all the rage now. The girls had told her they carried little vibrating bullets in their handbags so they could pop it in and get themselves going, anytime, anywhere. And apparently, it was now okay to discuss your preferences and pleasures with virtual strangers. She didn't know if she could ever be open enough to discuss intimate details of her sex life with anyone except Sam. Even Byron and Annabel only got the bare facts, but that way seemed to suit them all. They didn't share with her, and she didn't share with them.

She stayed for a while longer, enjoying the company, so different from her normal routine. They told stories of one-night stands, affairs with married men, and even one case of a quickie with a stranger in a train station while waiting for the last train home.

"So, do none of you want to settle down?" she asked.

"Are you serious?" Jan took a sip of her cocktail. "I wouldn't waste my time settling down here with an Irish fella. They're all right for a bit of stress relief, but I wouldn't marry one."

"Why?" Cathy was genuinely interested in what these women saw as their long-term relationship goals.

"I'll be heading out of the country," Michelle said. "Probably to the Emirates or Saudi Arabia. Somewhere like that. That's where the money is, and that's where you meet the really wealthy fellas. Sons of oil tycoons, royalty, business men, and sheiks. Men who could drop the money on a Ferrari and not bat an eyelid. That's the kind of man I'm going to marry."

Michelle was gorgeous enough that she probably would snag the eye of a handsome young prince, if she ever travelled to one of those places. The other girls were stunning, too, but it saddened Cathy that this was the attitude of Ireland's young women. Fair-haired men, with freckles or pasty-white skin, were no longer good enough for these metropolitan ladies. *What's wrong with a rich farmer?* She said goodbye and made her way back to her room.

She tiptoed in, expecting Annabel to be taking a nap. Instead, she found her pacing the floor with her mobile phone stuck to her ear.

"It doesn't work like that." She held an index finger up when Cathy raised a questioning eyebrow. Her face was like thunder. "Don't tell me you don't know how to do this, Gemma. This is your job. It should have been finished days ago. Why are you only looking at the files and discovering the problem now?"

Cathy went to the bathroom, giving Annabel some privacy, but she could still hear her strong voice through the closed door.

"Don't try to pass this off as my mistake, Gemma. I have emails to prove you knew about all this before yesterday. Now, get your head down and do the work. I don't care if it takes all weekend. That report is to be with Ms Connolly first thing Monday morning or my ass is fired."

Cathy thought she was finished, but then the shouting continued. "I'm not bullying you, Gemma. This is work. You've had it for days. This wouldn't be a problem if you'd done it when I asked. I'm not taking the rap for this."

Annabel paused, probably to listen to Gemma. "If the reports aren't ready for Monday, you'll be doing the explaining, not me. This is your problem now. Deal with it. And don't ring me again," she yelled. Then there was silence.

Cathy emerged from the bathroom to be faced with a pale, shaking Annabel. "What was that all about?" She poured a glass of sparkling water and handed it to her friend.

Annabel gulped down the drink. She took a deep breath and shook herself out of her aggressive state. "Do you remember the new girl I was telling you about? Gemma?"

Cathy nodded.

"Well, she's only gone and dropped me right into the shit." She finished her water and poured more.

"I couldn't help overhearing," Cathy said. "But surely there's some wriggle room on those reports?"

"There isn't," Annabel snapped. "My job's on the line if those figures don't add up."

"Maybe this Gemma made a mistake? Read the deadline wrong? These things happen, Annie."

"She didn't make a mistake, Cathy. Stop sticking up for her. She does this all the bloody time, licking up to managers, dumping crappy workloads on us mere mortals. Then, when the work she's supposed to be doing doesn't meet its deadline, we're the gobshites who end up in the firing line, because it's our names on the files."

Cathy tried to reason with her, but it was like waving a red flag at an already raging bull.

"Just shut up, Cathy, you've no idea what you're talking about. You're an idiot if you think there's nothing sinister going on here. She's trying to get me fired. I know she is. Gemma's a sneaky little bitch, twisting everything to make it look like someone else is at fault."

Her pacing had increased into a frenzied march around the room, and Cathy thought she'd wear a path in the carpet. Placing herself right in the firing line, she grabbed her by the arms. "Stop this, Annie. Stop it! I know that's not you speaking to me like that. It's crazy, stressed Annabel, who has lost control and is unable to see the wood for the trees."

Annabel shook her off and started pacing again, this time taking it slower. "It's not as simple as that," she said, turning to look at Cathy. "Gemma has been causing me trouble since the day she started. I've no idea why she dislikes me so much."

Cathy didn't know what she could do to help her friend. She just shrugged and held her hands out to let Annabel know she was there for her.

"One thing's for certain," Annabel continued, "I'm not going to lose my job just because that jumped-up little bitch thinks she can sail through life on her looks, sleeping her way to the top, and not an honest day's work done from one week to the next."

She stopped and focused on Cathy, her eyes softening as she stepped forward. "I'm sorry, Cathy, I shouldn't have said that to you. I'm just wound up to ninety, that's all. I know I sound like a right bitch, but you shouldn't be the one getting the brunt of it." She hugged Cathy.

Cathy hugged her back, Annabel's body still shaking from her outburst. "You need to calm down, Annabel, or you'll end up with an ulcer. There is nothing you can do about that report now, so let this Gemma one stress about it for a few hours, and you try to relax and enjoy yourself."

"I know, it's just she winds me up something rotten. I've enough to be worrying about with my own job, without babysitting someone else's too. I wish she would either cop the hell on, or piss off to wherever she came from."

"Look, you've said your piece, threatened her to within an inch of her life on the phone, so there's nothing more you can do now." She massaged her friend's shoulders. "Let's go for a walk, and later on you can check up on her again, just to put your mind at ease."

Annabel stretched her neck, rolling her head from side to side, and Cathy saw some tension finally leaving her body. "Okay, I'll give her a chance to redeem herself, but mark my words, Cathy, if she fucks this up, I'll be wearing a Gemma-shaped overcoat before long."

Cathy leaned back. "Jesus, Annabel, I know you're my friend, and I love you to bits, but you are kind of a bitch. Did you know that?"

Annabel shrugged, a hint of a smile lifting the darkness from her eyes. "I'm well aware of my reputation, but that's reserved strictly for those outside my friend zone. If you ever need me to fight your corner, kid, just give me a call."

"I'll keep that in mind," Cathy said, "along with a note to self, to never piss you off so badly that you'll be wearing my skin as a fashion accessory. Come on, grab your real coat and we'll go rescue Byron from Lou Lou. Let's go do some sightseeing in this beautiful old city."

Annabel groaned and shook her body out again. "I'd prefer to visit the whiskey distillery."

"That's the stress talking, Annie. And you know Lou Lou will poop a canary if we turn up at the hair and make-up session full of Ireland's finest malt."

"All right, all right, I suppose a bit of culture wouldn't go amiss, but first I need to prise Byron out of that bunny boiler's clutches." She grabbed her coat from the back of a chair and headed out of the room.

***

After the make-up and hair session had them all styled to within an inch of their lives, Lou Lou instructed everyone into the little black dresses and heels she had insisted they wear. Everyone except Byron donned a uniform look, while the bride-to-be stuck out in her fire engine red dress.

All the girls gathered in Byron and Lou Lou's room, having been told to meet there for pre, pre-dinner drinks.

As they entered, Lou Lou handed each hen a small paper bag. "Party favours, girls, and it's compulsory to wear them all night."

Annabel groaned, not even pretending to be excited by the mystery of it all. Cathy could tell she wasn't in the mood for fun and frivolity, obviously still upset about her problem with her work colleague. Right now, it looked like all she wanted was to get drunk and wallow in self-pity. *I'll have to keep an eye on her.*

Gasps of confusion and surprise filled the room as each girl opened her paper bag.

"Where's all the willies?" Michelle asked, holding up a long string of fake pearls.

"And the fruity flavoured condoms?" Jan added beneath a face full of black-feather boa.

Lou Lou shook her head in disgust. "It's not that type of hen party, ladies. Byron specifically said 'no smut', so I had to change the theme." She looked around at the many blank faces. "I finally settled on a more sophisticated, elegant approach to the traditional hen do."

"But what's all this?" Cathy asked as she inspected what could only be described as a child-size garter belt, complete with fake jewels and a feather.

"That," Lou Lou said, taking the item from Cathy and placing it neatly over her recently styled hair, "goes on your head. Wear it like a headband, ladies, and try not to mess the hair."

Lou Lou looked around again, everyone still none the wiser as to what they were supposed to be. She raised her hands and cleared her throat. "We are going to be 1920s flapper girls." She delivered this with a flourish.

"We are going to be what?" a slurred voice asked from the back.

Lou Lou giggled like a schoolgirl. "Oh, you're all too young to appreciate it, but let me explain."

Byron turned to Annabel. "What the…? She's the same age as us? What's she talking about?"

"Sssh," Annabel hissed.

Cathy smiled at that. For once Annabel actually looked interest in something Lou Lou had to say.

"America in the 1920s was a time of the first youth rebellion," Lou Lou explained. "The new woman was well and truly here. Flapper girls smoked and drank, just like men, and danced the night away with reckless abandonment." She finished to a shocked silence.

"Who swapped the sergeant major with this little devil?" Sarah asked, going straight up to Lou Lou's face and looking into her eyes, nose to nose. "Who are you and what have you done with Lou Lou Fleming?"

The rest of the girl's googled *flapper girl* to see exactly what Lou Lou was talking about.

"Oh my God, this is amazing," Byron said, as she and Cathy looked at pictures of girls in black dresses, feather boas, pearls, and a striking headband. "This is the perfect thing for us." She gestured around as everyone arranged accessories to match the pictures. "Look at us, we look brilliant. This was a fantastic idea, Lou Lou. Thank you." She beamed from ear to ear, her delight obvious to all.

"Line up, line up, girls." Lou Lou was back in charge. "I want to take a photograph." Sally, Natasha, Jan, Michelle, Nicola, Brenda, Helen, Annmarie, and Sarah, all crowded around, linking arms and raising glasses, as Byron, Annabel, and Cathy knelt in front, all ready for a group photo.

Lou Lou raised the camera and shouted above the excited din, "Okay, ladies, on my count – one, two, three, willies!" She snapped off a number of photos, capturing twelve shocked and stunned expressions.

The women exploded in a cackle of riotous screams. "Okay, okay, let me take that one again," Lou Lou shouted. "None of you were smiling."

Byron jumped up and pulled Lou Lou into the picture, then, attaching the camera to a selfie stick, captured the perfect photo of all her clucking hens.

"Come on, girls, it's time to party, party, party!" Nicola sang, topping up empty glasses while dancing around the room.

Glasses clinked and vodka-jelly shots disappeared into hungry bellies. Brenda popped the cork on a bottle of pink champagne and poured generous helpings for everyone.

"This is the pre, pre-dinner drinks, right?" Cathy shouted over the loud chatter in the room.

Annabel nodded, helping herself to another glass of champagne.

"God love us all," Cathy said, sipping her drink, not wanting to get drunk while it was still so early. She watched as Byron laughed and joked with her friends, relieved the weekend had turned itself around. Her initial expectation hadn't been good, but now she was actually enjoying herself. She had to admit, Lou Lou's 1920s theme had saved the day. Without it they would have been identical to every other hen party on the razz that weekend.

By the time they hit Langton's nightclub, half the pubs in the city knew of their existence. Many of the boa's had been plucked almost bare by enquiring hands, and one or two of the girls had to make running repairs to their pearl necklaces, but the Dublin flapper girls were the talk of the town. They were taking Kilkenny by storm.

Stag parties wanted to party with them, and tourists wanted them in their photographs. Drunk men tried to grab a handful of ass, inquiring about the chances of a shag later. As the night went on, the drinks got smaller, but stronger, until finally, Cathy felt she could have no more. She swayed in slow motion to a fast-beat song on the dancefloor in Langton's, overwhelmed with tiredness as she tried to stay awake. Ten minutes earlier, someone banging on the door of the toilet had woken her up. She needed her bed.

She gestured over to Byron, shouting her goodbyes, letting her know she was done for the night.

"Ah, don't go," Byron said, gyrating between two dressed-up cowboys.

"I'm done, By. Sorry, I need my bed." She kissed her cheeks and eyed up the two guys beside her. "Behave yourself."

Byron laughed, "Not a chance." She nodded to the two cowboys, both continuing to dance. "Why would I settle for a man who dresses in a costume, when I have a real-life superhero waiting for me to marry him?"

Cathy hugged her. "Okay, I'm going now. I'll see you tomorrow."

Annabel took Cathy by the arm, steading her before leaning in to Byron. "I'm going, too. I'll make sure she gets back to the hotel okay."

"Bye, girls. See you tomorrow," Byron shouted over the music, waving them goodbye with handfuls of blown kisses.

Annabel took Cathy by the hand. "Let's get you out of here and into the fresh air." She lead Cathy through the packed club, and out to the waiting town car.

51

Before they reached the hotel, Cathy couldn't take the pain any longer, her stomach flipping over as a wave of nausea hit her. She flapped the air with one hand, the other clamped over her mouth, then slapped Annabel's lap. "Annie!"

"Stop the car," Annabel shouted at the driver, jumping out as the car pulled in. Cathy fumbled with the handle, and was about to hurl there and then when Annabel opened the door and she stumbled out of the car and over to a bank of hedges.

Her dinner and the night's drinks hit the ditch with a splat. "Oh, Jesus Christ, I'm dying!"

Annabel handed her a bottle of water. "Here, honey, rinse your mouth out with this." She held Cathy's hair off her sweaty face as she gargled and spat out the water. "Do you think you're done, or do you need to go again?"

Cathy straightened and wiped her mouth on the back of her hand. "I think I'm okay now. Those chicken wings were sitting on me funny all night."

"Okay, let's go," Annabel said, guiding her back to the car. "Come on, Cathy, you can make it. The hotel's only five minutes from here."

Cathy let herself be guided into the back of the car. She was that helpless, all she was missing was the child seat. *Never again.*

Annabel assured the driver that Cathy wasn't drunk. "She just has a stomach bug."

Cathy caught his admonishing eye in the rear-view mirror and looked down at her shaking hands.

"I don't care what she had," he said, "but if she gets sick in the back of this car, you're paying for it. And here's the pricelist if you don't believe me."

"Just drive," Annabel bit out, putting an arm around Cathy. "Babe, do your best to keep it in until we reach the hotel."

They made it to their room without incident, but once inside the stuffy room, Cathy couldn't hold it any longer and sprinted for the bathroom.

"I've got a feeling," Annabel said, standing behind her, "that it's going to be a very long night."

Cathy retched and gagged as Annabel tied her long blond hair back from her face and wiped her brow. *This is what true friendship is about.*

6th April

6th April

Sunday

"Oh, sweet baby Jesus. Never again."

Cathy eased one eye open, followed by the other when she was sure her head wouldn't explode.

A muffled voice came from under the duvet on the other bed. "Are you all right, Cathy?"

"I will be in a minute, 'cause I'll be dead."

"Ah, you didn't have that much to drink," Annabel said, throwing back the duvet.

"I know," Cathy agreed, barely able to move without her stomach heaving. "It must have been the dodgy chicken wings—"

"And the vodka!"

"Okay, and the vodka. You know I can't drink vodka. It sends me loopy. Why did you let me drink vodka, Annabel? This is all your fault." She rubbed her head and bent to ease the nausea radiating through her abdomen.

Annabel laughed, but stopped as sudden as she'd started. "What the hell were we doing in that nightclub, anyway?"

Cathy groaned at the pictures seeping into her head – fuzzy visuals of the hens on tour, all dressed as 1920s flapper girls, mingling enthusiastically with a stag party of half-stripped cowboys.

"I'm having flashbacks, Annabel, and it's not good. There were drunken men involved."

"Don't worry, you were a good girl. It's that other one who needs to take a long hard look at herself."

"Who, Lou Lou? Why, what did she do?" Cathy flopped back onto the bed, relieved that even though she felt dreadful, she hadn't made too much of a show of herself.

"Well, let's just say, for all her squeaky-clean dictatorship ways, she needs to rein in her slutty alter ego when she's out and about and there's drink involved."

Cathy gasped, unable to believe how the mighty had fallen. "No way. Did she do something?"

Annabel frowned. "I can't believe you've no memory of last night's shenanigans. All Lou Lou was short of doing was mounting the John Wayne lookalike, right there in the middle of the dancefloor. Security had to throw them both out. The words *indecent behaviour* were being bandied about by the club owners. When we followed them out, she'd disappeared with the bloke." She laughed to herself. "Probably rode him off into the sunset."

"Oh my God." Cathy couldn't believe it. "What happened then?"

"Well, I think someone finally got her on the mobile and made sure she was okay, but I'd say there'll be a very sorry-looking Lou Lou Fleming keeping her head down today. I'd be surprised if she even shows her face."

Cathy chuckled, but then her throat tightened and her stomach churned. She sprang out of bed and ran for the bathroom, just about making it to the pot. Annabel rubbed her back as she retched.

"Ugh, what the hell is wrong with me, Annie?"

"I don't think it's the drink, Cathy. Seriously, you didn't have that much. I think you're just worn out and stressed. Still, hard to believe one night out has taken such a toll on you."

Cathy left the bathroom, perspiration clinging to her face and neck. "That feckin' vomiting bug was going around the school during the week. It might be that. Anyway, I'm going to get cleaned up and head home. Sam is coming over later and I have to collect the kids." She started packing up last night's clothes and make-up, pulling out a fresh pair of jeans and a t-shirt for after her shower.

"Thank God Mum has the children. I couldn't face Gary in this state."

"Listen, Cathy," Annabel said, her voice quiet, "I'm sorry again about yesterday. I really didn't mean to speak to you like that. But if it's any consolation, I've been thinking about what you said. Maybe I am being too hard on the girl."

Cathy crossed the room and hugged her friend. "Mind yourself, Annie. I love you, you know that, right?"

Annabel remained silent, just nodding into her shoulder.

"I know there's something bothering you and I really wish you'd talk to me properly about it, preferably when you haven't just had a blazing row with your work colleague, and I'm next in the firing line."

"It's nothing, Cathy, just some silly stuff getting in on me, and I'm letting it fester. But last night really did help. Turned out to be a great night in the end." She untangled herself from Cathy's embrace. "Go get yourself ready and I'll pop over to Byron's room to let her know we're heading off. We'll get a McDonalds' drive-through on the way home. Leave the others to their hangovers, yeah?"

Cathy gagged, her face going cold at the thought of a Big Mac and chips. She only just made it back to the bathroom before hurling up a good chunk of stomach.

"Okay, maybe just coffee for you," Annabel said, once again holding Cathy's hair out of the firing line.

***

After dropping Cathy home, Annabel drove the short distance from Wicklow to Greystones to see her mother.

"Hi, Mum," she called out as she pushed in the front door of her childhood home. She was instantly surrounded by the smell of hot scones and brown bread. Her mother loved to bake, and it was moments like this that brought Annabel straight back to her childhood – of running in the door from school, to be enclosed in a deep hug of spices, wondering what treat her mother had in store for her then.

A voice from further down the hall brought her back as her mother emerged from the kitchen to greet her. "Annabel, how lovely to see you, my dear."

"Mum, how are you doing?" She swallowed back an unexpected surge of guilt-tinged self-pity and gave her a quick peck on the cheek. They moved into the cosy living room, where Annabel headed straight to the high-backed winged chair in the corner.

"What brings you down here today?" Her mother's tone was gentle, as if she sensed there was something bothering her. The woman never missed a thing.

"Ah, I'm just back from Byron's hen weekend in Kilkenny. I dropped Cathy home and thought I'd pay you a quick visit. I haven't actually seen you in person for a while, Mum. How are you keeping?"

"I'm grand, love, just grand. And don't you be fretting, sure you're on the phone every day, and since I've got the hang of that Skype thing, well, you're hardly off it. But in saying all that, it really is lovely to see you."

"You too, Mum." She smiled and waited, knowing there was more coming.

"You look tired, though. You're probably busy running around all the time, doing too much, not looking after yourself properly. I bet last night was a late one, eh? What with it being a hen party and all that."

Annabel sighed. Sometimes it was easier to communicate with her mother over Skype or the phone. She could invent excuses and make a quick exit, something that was much harder to do in person.

"No, it wasn't too bad. I was with Cathy most of the night. She wasn't feeling great, so I ended up taking her back to the hotel at a reasonable hour."

Her mother's eyes narrowed. "What's up with *poor* Cathy?"

Annabel ignored the barb. "I think all the stress of how things are between her and Sam is beginning to take its toll on her. She's completely worn out, and not handling it very well, if you ask me."

Her mother raised her head and sniffed, conveying her distaste of Cathy without having to say anything. Annabel accepted how she was – how she didn't approve of divorce, or having children out of wedlock, or any of the *new-fangled* ideas the young people of today thought was acceptable behaviour. She'd been careful to never mention that Jean Luc spent most nights at her apartment when he was in

Ireland, rarely sleeping in his own bed. Her mother would not approve.

"Well, darling, don't you be worrying about all that business. Concentrate on yourself for a change. How is Jean Luc? Is he still on the scene? I liked him, even with all his airs and graces. He was a grand chap, so he was."

"He's fine, Mum. He's in the Middle East on business at the moment. Abu Dhabi, actually. He'll be home soon, I hope."

"Oh, very fancy. But I have to say, I don't really care for the culture over there. Very strict with their women, I believe. And the weather? Sure that heat would kill you, even on a winter's day."

Annabel smiled at the image of her mother prancing her way through the air-conditioned hotels of Abu Dhabi, refusing to step outside for fear she might break into a sweat. The woman was indeed one cool cucumber.

"Well, hopefully he'll be back in Ireland in the next week or so. I miss him when he's gone."

Her mother's sharp look caught her off guard.

"So you are living together then?"

"What? No, Mum, of course we're not. He has his own place and I have mine. We're just seeing each other, that's all. Anyway, any chance of a cup of tea? I'm parched after the long drive." Better to have her mother make tea than be stuck hearing about the sins of living, or lying with a man outside the bounds of holy matrimony. She didn't have the energy for that particular lecture today.

"Relax there now and I'll go and pop the kettle on. I made scones this morning. I had a funny feeling there would be visitors today."

Her mother scurried off into the kitchen while Annabel stayed in the living room, guilt-ridden by her last remark. She tried to visit when she could, but since her father's passing two years ago, she found it difficult to be in the house. Her heart ached each time she remembered his hearty laugh and that special fragrance he always used. Tears welled as she stood and looked around. She picked up a photo from the sideboard. Mum, Dad, Annabel, and Michael, her brother, camping in some god-forsaken back-of-beyond. The photo captured smiles as wide as the River Liffey. In the background she could just make out an old-style camping stove boiling up a pot of water for tea, while brown and orange sleeping bags hung from a makeshift clothesline, airing in the summer breeze. Her childhood, summed up with one click.

She ran her thumb around her father's face and blinked a tear away. *I miss you so much, Dad.* "Oh, why can't you be still here?" she whispered, before setting the photo back in its place. She took a deep breath, wiped her face dry, and followed her mother into the kitchen to help with the tea.

Later, when she got home, she'd take out and re-read some of the diaries she'd kept from her dad's belongings. It always helped her to feel close to him again, but for now, she would give her mum all the love she could, while she still could.

7th April

Monday

As she loaded the dishwasher after the school run, Cathy couldn't believe how tired she felt. She was still recovering from the hen party, and now Sam was here, the best part of the night before had been spent in some compromising positions. But this fatigue wasn't the happy, satisfied, floating-on-air kind of tiredness. It was dark and achy, and seeped right into the marrow of her bones, and made her want to hibernate for the next two weeks. Once she'd tidied the kitchen, she climbed the stairs and crawled back into bed.

Sam rolled over onto his back as her movements woke him. She rested her head on his chest, feeling his strong arms wrap around her, his soft kiss grazing her temple.

"Morning, babe," he mumbled.

She inhaled his musky scent – so masculine – and snuggled closer, listening to the steady beat of his heart as she relaxed into a semi-slumber. It didn't take long before she drifted into a deep, snore-inducing sleep, protected in the arms of the man she loved.

A ringing phone woke her later. She patted around, eyes closed, until she located the offending item on the bedside locker.

"Hello."

"Cathy, I need a favour."

"Of course you do," she said, regretting that she'd answered without checking the caller ID. Gary, her ex-husband.

"No, wait, Cathy, seriously, I need you to help me out a bit this week – switch around a few of the days I'm supposed to have the kids."

She covered her eyes, irritation surging through her. "Fine, Gary, whatever you want. What's the excuse this time?"

"Something came up, I won't be able to take the children on Tuesday or Thursday, as arranged...or at the weekend."

"Ah, Gary, are you serious?" She sat up. "When are they going to get to see you? You can't keep doing this. You know they get terribly upset when things change. They need a routine, Gary. They need stability, not this chopping and changing whenever the mood suits you or you're able to fit them into your busy schedule of ducking and diving."

She knew the last bit was a cheap shot because, despite all his faults, Gary adored the twins and tried his best when it came to their welfare.

"Cathy, look, I know it's short notice, but I'll make it up to them, and you. I promise."

"What is it then? What is it this time that's so urgent it just has to be done today and not a minute later?"

"I have a bit of business that needs looking after," he said, so smooth it sounded well-practiced.

"It might lead to something a bit more permanent, Cathy. I can't turn my nose up at this."

She sighed through gritted teeth, feeling like she was stuck between a rock and a hard place. Since last year, when Gary had screwed up bigtime by losing his barman's job, he'd been temping his way around Dublin, with the odd under-the-counter *business* deal thrown in.

She'd been troubled at the time that he didn't care about being fired, but she'd then found out, through the grapevine, that he'd received a golden handshake of sorts, and that money had kept him going for the first few months. It was only since Christmas, after the seasonal work in bars and clubs had dried up, that he'd started stressing about money again.

"This had better be worth it, Gary. You need to get your act together and get yourself sorted. It's not fair on the children." She knew how to hit where it hurt. "Millie and Jack are only six, Gary. They miss you when you're not around. They don't understand."

"I know, Cathy." His words held a harder edge now, and she guessed he was in no mood for one of her lectures about good parenting.

"Right, well, good luck with whatever it is you're doing. If it's illegal, I don't want to know, but if you could possibly spare a few moments some evening, maybe you'd give the children a quick ring, just to say hello. That would be great."

"Don't be smart, Cathy," he said, and she could almost hear him biting his tongue, wanting to be done with this conversation.

"Next week, Gary, the children are on their Easter holidays. Right?"

"Yeah, I didn't forget. It's written on the calendar, smartarse."

"So maybe you can let me know if it suits you to have your children come stay with you, their father, for a couple of days. What do you think?" She was in full fighting form now, wide awake and ready to tear strips off anyone who got in her way. "And listen to me now, this can't keep happening. It's not fair on them. They feel abandoned every time you let them down, and it's me who has to deal with the aftermath of your careless attitude."

"All right, Cathy, Jesus Christ, I got the message the first time." She knew he was likely to explode if she kept pushing him. "I'll ring them later to explain, and don't you be worrying, Cathy," he said, almost too sweetly, "you'll have plenty of time to look after yourself and the wonderful Sam soon enough. See ya around!"

Staring at the blank screen, she wondered if she'd heard him correctly. "Asshole." She flung the phone down and pulled back the covers.

"Who's an asshole?" Sam asked, entering the room with two mugs of tea.

"Gary." She nodded at the phone as she reached for a mug. "He can't take the children again this week, or at the weekend."

Sam sat beside her on the bed. "What's he up to?"

"Oh, I don't know. Some scam or dodgy deal, I'd bet." She sipped her sweet tea. "But it was the way he said that I'd soon have plenty of time to look after myself and the 'wonderful Sam' that's bugging me the most. What the fuck does he mean by that?"

Tension thumped through her temples as she processed his words. "Is he thinking that he can take full custody of my children? Well, he will have a fucking war on his hands. Over my dead body." She placed the cup on the locker for fear she'd drop it. "He must be bloody delusional. What judge is going to give that scheming, cheating, lying bastard custody of any children?"

She stopped then, realising what she'd just said and how Sam was looking at her. "I mean, he's a good dad to them. I know for a fact he would never let any harm come near them." Then she thought of everything that had happened. "But that doesn't take away from the fact that he, as a person, is the most selfish, self-centred bollox I know. He'd never give up his schemes and womanising to look after Millie and Jack. He didn't give those dirty little secrets up when we were married. Is he on drugs or—"

"Cathy, love, he's winding you up."

"What?"

He handed back her cup of tea. "Look, you probably gave him hell on the phone just now, right?"

"He deserved it. He thinks he can just—"

"He's just trying to piss you off. The guy knows which buttons to press with you, Cathy. He does it every time you let fly, and you take it."

She gulped her tea, taking time to calm herself and consider what Sam was saying.

"You know him better than me, Cathy, even though I've had enough dealings with him to last a lifetime, but you know what he's like, it's all just words." He put his arm around her shoulder and hugged her to him. "There's not a hope in hell of Gary ever fighting you for full custody of the twins. Never. He knows exactly how to wind you up, and that's all he's doing."

She nodded and chewed her lip. He was right, of course. Spot on. "I'm sick of him, Sam. Only for the children, I wish he'd just piss off somewhere else and leave us all alone." She'd considered a move away many times, but knew how devastated the children would be, not being able to see their dad. Perhaps when they were older and able to travel on their own, it might be an option.

She smiled to herself. *Just because he's an asshole, doesn't mean I can't play dirty too.*

Sam leaned away and eyed her. "What are you grinning at?"

"Oh, just some innocent plans that would make the Wicked Witch look like Mary Poppins." She let out an evil cackle, bringing on a fit of coughing.

"Come here." Sam pulled her to him. "Let me help you with all that restrictive clothing." He lifted her t-shirt over her head and unhooking the pink lacy bra underneath.

Cathy shoved him onto his back, before she rolled away and jumped off the bed.

"Oh, you want it rough, do you?" He jumped up, grabbing for her as she made a run for it.

"No, Sam," she mumbled, one hand covering her mouth as she dashed towards the en-suite bathroom. She caught the look of confusion and concern on his face before she slammed the door shut. "Don't come in here," she said, kneeling to puke into the toilet bowl.

"Can I come in now?" he asked, a few minutes later.

"Oh, Sam," she groaned as he reached her side and cleared her wet hair from her sweaty brow. She couldn't prevent the tears coming – damming on her lashes before overflowing onto her cheeks. Sam pulled her from a kneeling position into his lap, then wrapped his arms around her.

"Do you feel a bit better?" He rocked her back and forth, the movement gentle and peaceful after the violence of retching and gagging. She rested her head on his chest as he wiped her tearstained face with a damp towel. "Was it the tea that made you sick? Do you think the milk was gone off?"

"No." She burst out crying again – hearty, heavy sobs that took ages to subside and enable her to speak again. "No, I don't think it was the tea. I think… I… Oh, shit." Taking a deep, shaky breath, she closed her eyes and decided the best thing to do was spit it out.

"Sam, I think I might be… Well, you know… Pregnant." She opened her eyes to look at him.

He stared at her, his mouth open. "Oh."

8th April

Tuesday

Sam sat holding Cathy's hand, doing his best to remain patient as he looked around the busy waiting room. Elderly gentlemen read out-of-date magazines, while stressed-out parents endeavoured to keep children under control, all hoping it would be their turn next. He smiled at a young mother carrying a tiny baby in a sling against her chest. Only when she smiled weirdly back at him did he realise he'd been staring at her for several minutes.

He smiled back in an effort to put her at ease. "How old is he?"

"Eight weeks," she answered.

"And he's doing well, is he? I mean, he's not sick or anything? I'd be worried about that, with him being so young and all." Cathy looked at him, but he was on a roll. "I suppose that's why you're here, getting him checked out? Can't be too careful, can you? Not with babies, anyway."

The young mother just stared back.

"What is it?" he asked. "A sniffle? A bit of a cold? I'm sure he'll be okay. He'll be grand." He looked at Cathy, who'd squeezed his hand a bit too tight.

"What?"

"Shut up," she whispered.

"What? But I'm only—"

71

"You're making her uncomfortable, Sam. The baby is probably here for vaccinations. Stop freaking her out."

He folded his arms as Cathy smiled across at the young woman, who rolled her eyes and nodded towards him.

"Yes, I'm here for the two-month vaccination. And just to let you know, he's actually a she. Her name is Megan."

Heat flushed into Sam's face. "Oh, sorry about that. You know how they all look the same at that age. Just babies, the image of each other. Don't really know how the doctor can tell them apart at the hospital."

Megan's mother looked away, her mouth a thin line.

"I'd say parents go home with the wrong babies all the time, much more than they let you know, actually."

"Sam, love," Cathy said between gritted teeth, "shut up. Stop talking. Now!"

The waiting room fell into an eerie silence – even the phones at reception stopped buzzing. All eyes were on Sam.

All he could do was shrug. "Sorry, Cathy. I'm…nervous." He threw an apologetic smile towards the young mother, now clutching Megan to her chest. Cathy rubbed his arm – soft gentle strokes up and down.

"Relax, Sam. This is just a quick chat with the doctor. Maybe a blood test, or something."

He let out a slow breath, trying to steady his nerves. "Right, but do you think we'll know for certain today, if you're…you know?" He raised his eyebrows, almost afraid to speak the word.

"I'm not sure," she answered, "but after yesterday's disaster, this is the best way to find out for certain."

He thought back to yesterday morning, when Cathy had dropped the bombshell, right into the middle of his world.

"Sam, I think I might be… Well, you know… Pregnant."

After staring at each other for a long moment, he'd helped her off the bathroom floor and led her to the side of the bed.

"Cathy, I didn't…" He'd stopped, unable to think straight. "I don't… How could you be?"

She'd shook her head, as confused as him.

He couldn't believe it. His voice rose as he tried to figure out how it could be true. "We've barely seen each other for the past few months and, Jesus, unless technology has really advanced, I'm pretty sure you can't get pregnant during phone sex."

"I know, I know, Sam," she cried. "And stop shouting at me. I don't know how this happened, either. It's just, well…I don't—" She stopped, stared

73

at him, then her face turned red and she shoved him away from her. "Are you actually suggesting, Sam O'Keefe, that I've been cheating on you? That I've been carrying on with someone else behind your back? Because, if that's what you're saying, you can go and—"

"That's not what I'm saying, Cathy." He jumped up, still confused but now realising what he'd implied. A shiver ran across his shoulders as cold sweat prickled his forehead. He looked down at her. "I didn't mean it like that." He wasn't liking where this conversation was going. Not for one second was he suggesting she'd cheated on him. It had never even crossed his mind. "I'd never…"

"Then what exactly are you saying, Sam?"

"I don't know. Well, actually, I do," he said, his mind grasping something resembling clarity. "The logistics, Cathy. How could you be pregnant? I'm never here." He turned a half circle, his hands out. "And even when I am here, it's only for a night or two. And for God's sake, we're always so careful, right?" His voice rose again, "You are on the pill, right?" He watched in horror when her face crumpled.

"I don't know what to tell you, Sam," she said through the tears. "And stop blaming me. There was two of us going at it like rabbits, as far as I can remember." She stood up, visibly shaking as she tried to put distance between them.

Then she stopped, as if remembering something important. "And you listen to me, Mister. The pill doesn't always do the job. For your information, there are thousands of kids running around out there as a result of such failures. It's not totally unheard of, you know." She pointed a trembling finger at him. "And another thing, I only said I *think* I might be pregnant. You idiot. I'm not even sure. It could be a false alarm, for all we know."

Sam held his breath, careful to choose the right words. "Okay, then tell me now, what makes you *think* you might be pregnant?"

She had the good grace to look ashamed when she answered his direct question. "Well, my period is late."

"Really? How late?"

"Over a week," she answered, counting her fingers. "Actually, no, more like ten days."

Sam's face went cold. "Jesus, Cathy, why didn't you tell me?"

"I didn't know," she said, one hand on her forehead, "I didn't actually realise. What with the hen party and being away for two days, and then the excitement of you coming home, and with the kids…" She trailed off, her hands out, palms up.

Sam pointed at her stomach. "But surely you keep an eye on that sort of thing?" Even saying that petrified him – it was way too personal. *What if she start's explaining it all?*

She stared at him as if he'd sprouted a second nose. "Of course I do. What do you take me for?" She paced back and forth, wringing her hands together. "I finished my pill, and…normally it takes a couple of days for things to, you know, kick in?" She gestured with both hands to her pelvis. "But then it didn't, and I forgot, and the days got away from me, and then I started feeling sick last week…"

Another shock for Sam. "What? Were you sick before today?"

"Yes, a few mornings last week," she said, "but I just thought it was to do with that vomiting bug going around the school, or maybe I was run down, or fecking-well stressed or something." She groaned and shook both hands out. "I was having cramps as well so I thought my period was on the way."

She continued to pace back and forth, working the hangnail on her thumb. "Then I was sick at the hen party, but I thought it was the chicken wings, or the vodka."

Sam couldn't believe what he was hearing.

Cathy stopped pacing, right in front of him, and looked at him with watery eyes. "Sam, it was only now, this morning, when I was throwing up in the bathroom, that I spotted the pill packet for next month and put two and two together."

She continued to speak directly to him, her gaze unwavering. "I've counted up. I'm ten days late."

Sam swallowed. "Oh shit."

"Shit, shit, shit, and crap," she said. "Oh, sweet Jesus, Sam, this can't be happening. What the hell am I going to do?"

"Okay, hang on." He guided her to sit beside him on the bed. "You said you only *think* you might be pregnant, right?"

She nodded.

"Then…do you think you should do a test or something?" He'd pulled out the only option his brain would show him. "You said yourself that it felt like you were getting your… You know…" He held his hand out, as if weighing something invisible. "And if you had the cramps and stuff, well then maybe it's just stress that's holding it back – stopping it coming, or whatever."

His embarrassment had peaked. When it came to sex, he'd no problem getting to know every inch of Cathy's body, but discussing the intimate workings and possible faulty plumbing was a big no-no.

Cathy sighed, her shoulders becoming less rigid. "I'll get a test then." Sam caught a glimmer of hope in her eyes. "You're right," she said, "I'll do a test, and then we'll know, right?"

He nodded. "Right."

"And Sam, please don't freak out, okay?" She took his face in both hands. "I'm terrified enough as it is. I've no idea what to think with all of this."

He rested his head in her trembled hands, supporting them with his own.

"This is a pregnancy scare," she said. "Something all couples go through when they're having a bit of fun. It's almost like a rite of passage."

He pulled back, shaking his head. "A bit of fun? Cathy, this is not just a bit of fun."

She ducked her head before looking into his eyes. "Yes, I know, I know. I just meant—"

"No, Cathy, listen to me." He lifted her hands to his brow, then kissed them and took a deep breath. "I know things are difficult between us. Not that we're not getting on, but that I'm away in England, dealing with this Sorcha stuff. I can't give a hundred percent to the relationship." He took another breath, this one long and shaky. "But I have to tell you one thing, I am more in love with you now, even more than I was when you chased me through the airport last September. You told me that day that we needed to be together, even when there was an ocean between us. You were willing to call us a couple."

She remained silent while he poured his heart into his words. "I love your strength, your passion, everything about you, Cathy. You *are* my world now." He stopped to catch his breath, his face crumpling with the same emotions Cathy had seen last year when she almost lost him. "I thought I could let you go when I found out about Sorcha. Seriously, I thought it was the best thing for both of us. But you proved me wrong. You clung on, fought through it all, and wouldn't let me make the biggest mistake of my life by letting you go."

Cathy's cheeks were soaked from her tears. Sam pulled her to him, moulding her into his body. He used the corner of his shirt to dry her face, then rocked back and forth, relishing the closeness.

"Cathy, my love," he whispered, caressing the back of her head, "I'm in deep, deep, everlasting love with you. I'm here for the long haul, no matter what ingredients get thrown into the mix. This is it for me, and yes, I promise not to freak out, but only if you do, too."

Her eyes glistened as she nodded. "I promise."

He released the breath he'd been holding. "All right then, let's get this test sorted and see what's going on."

"Okay, but Sam…" She hesitated. "Will you do me a favour?"

His stomach lurched. *What're you going to ask me to do now?*

"Will you go into the chemist and get the test for me? I can't face it. The gossip if anyone sees me." She touched her blushing cheek. "No one knows you down here. You could be anyone."

He couldn't help grinning. "Yes, love, I'll go and get it, and then you can do your bit. And then we'll know."

She nodded again, wiping more tears from her cheeks.

Sam helped her and kissed her nose, hoping he was comforting her in some way, even though his stomach felt like a bagpipe being squeezed. It was difficult projecting an air of confidence and understanding, when in truth, he could give Cathy a run for her money on the vomit-meter. However, for now, he had to get his shit together, and get this test done. At least then they'd know.

***

Half an hour later he walked back into the house, white chemist bag in hand. Cathy was in the kitchen, pacing up and down the tiled floor, sipping on a pint of water.

"I'm scared, Sam." She put her glass on the counter and twirled her hair into a knot, then let it fall lose again. Sam sensed how nervous she was as she stood there looking like a dazed rabbit caught in headlights. He reached her in two strides and pulled her into a solid embrace.

"I'm scared too, Cathy," he confessed. "In fact, my nerves got the better of me while I was at the chemist."

She stiffened in his arms. "Oh, God, what did you do?"

He held her head close to his shoulder so she couldn't look at his face while he told the story. "Well, as I said, the nerves got the better of me." He scrunched his eyes closed as he remembered. "I couldn't find the test things. They had them hidden over in the corner, nearly on the floor. I've never been

80

near that side of a chemist's before, with all the female-hygiene products and stuff." He couldn't help shuddering.

Cathy tried to raise her head to look at him, but he held her fast, rubbing her shoulder and kissing her brow.

"Anyway, I must have done about five laps of the shop before the sales assistant came over to see if I needed any help." He cringed at the memory.

Cathy managed to work her head free and looked up into his face. With one eyebrow raised, she nodded, urging him on. "And...?"

"And...I may have started to speed-talk about how grateful I was for her help, and how it was my first time – not my first time having sex, but my first time buying a pregnancy test – and it was okay, because it wasn't just a one-night-stand shag or anything, but that we were in a semi-long-term, committed relationship, and even though we were both terrified, we loved each other very much, and that she shouldn't really judge you, or me, or anyone..." He couldn't say any more, the tightness in his throat making him feel like his tongue was swelling up.

Cathy remained silent for several moments, rapid blinks the only sign that she was computing what she'd just heard. "Oh, dear God, Sam."

"I know—"

"What is wrong with you?" she blurted out, her voice rising with every word. "Why would you say all that to someone? Jesus, I'm mortified." She stopped, her eyes widening. "Wait, tell me which chemist you went to so I'll know never to show my face near it again."

Sam shook his head. "Relax, love, they don't know the test is for you." He shrugged. "It's not like I had to give your name and address before I bought it." He watched her grab the test off the counter and walk out into the hall. She turned back when she reached the bottom of the stairs.

"Lucky for you I have an understanding nature. Otherwise, I swear, I'd string you up."

He swallowed behind his best smile. *God, what a nightmare.* He consoled himself with the thought that she seemed to be taking it in her stride. All he had to do now was wait for her to finish peeing on a stick.

Ten minutes later they stood looking at a blank test. Neither blue line had shown up, meaning the test had malfunctioned.

"Shit, what do we do now?" she asked.

"Do the other one in the box," Sam suggested. "It's a double pack."

She glared at him. "I've just been to the bathroom, I can't go again so soon."

He nodded. "I'll get you some water. Start drinking it now and you can try again in a while."

"Okay, but…" She stopped him leaving. "Look, it's nearly one o'clock. I have to collect the children from school, and I don't really want to do this with them around. I might wait 'til tonight to try again."

"That makes sense," he said, aware that he was still trembling inside.

***

They picked the children up from school and made them lunch. As they helped one child each with homework, Sam caught a look from Cathy that pushed back his turmoil. Though he was struggling, he winked at her and her returning smile made his day. Wouldn't be long now before the second test was done. The wait was killing him.

He brought Millie and Jack to the playground while Cathy looked after dinner. By seven that evening, they had both children fed, bathed, and tucked in bed waiting for a story.

Sam crept downstairs while Cathy got the children to sleep. He couldn't concentrate on the TV and flicked aimlessly through channel after channel, settling on a music station playing slow ballads. In no mood for dinner earlier, his empty stomach now growled, but he couldn't bring himself to eat a bite, afraid he might be sick. All day long he'd tried so hard to appear calm and relaxed in front of Cathy. His head was spinning with possibilities, both good and bad – each thought clamouring for space in the forefront of his mind, demanding immediate attention and dissection, making it impossible to think straight at all.

Unable to sit still for a second longer, he jumped up and went in search of Cathy. She needed to take that test. *I need to know.*

He ran into her outside the living-room door.

"I did it," she said, holding the white pregnancy test up.

"And…did it work?"

"It's negative," she answered, her face still as pale as it had been all day. Sam was sure he glimpsed sadness in her eyes.

"Negative? Really? So, what's the story then? Why are you late? Why are you sick?" If she answered, he didn't hear, buried as he was in the flood of emptiness and loss at the news. *What's going on? Surely I should be feeling relief.*

Cathy just shook her head, silent as she stood by his side, her eyes turned down.

"Negative," he said again. "Wow." He looked at her, her chest visibly shaking as she exhaled.

"I know this is so stupid," she whispered, wiping her eyes, "but I was so worried all day that the test would be positive. I had myself convinced that I was pregnant. But then, when the line didn't show up, I felt like I'd lost something precious, something I can never get back." She sobbed as she laid her head on his chest. "How can I be so upset about not having something that didn't even exist in the first place?"

"I know," he said, running a soothing hand over her head. "It's weird, I feel the same. I built myself up to hear bad news, and now it hasn't turned out that way, I realise it wouldn't have been bad news at all." He squeezed her to him. "I'm sorry, love."

She sniffed and wiped her face with her sleeve. "Well, I guess that's that." She untangled herself from his embrace and held the test up. "Time for the bin."

Sam's hair stiffened on his head, like an electric charge had been zapped into each one. He grabbed her hand as she stepped away and lifted the test towards him. *What the hell?* He looked at it, then at Cathy, then back again.

"Did you say there was no line on that test?"

"Yes, look." She took the test back and waved it between them.

He looked again at the little window, swallowing hard. *What the hell is going on? Can't she see what I'm seeing?*

"Cathy, there are two blue lines on this test."

"What? Wait…" She checked the result again and her mouth fell open. "They weren't there before." She shook the stick back and forth like a magic 8-ball, and Sam wondered for a moment if she was trying to see if the answer would change.

"Sam, oh my God, it changed!" She clasped the test to her chest, shaking her head in disbelief. "It didn't show up at first, but you're right. Sam, I'm pregnant. I'm pregnant!"

***

Sitting here now, at the doctor's office, Sam remembered how freaked out they'd both been last night. He'd held her close until the morning, lying awake trying to get his thoughts into some sort of order. Now they were here, in the last-chance saloon. This was the defining moment – when it would all change or stay the same. By the time they left here today, he would know if he was going to be a father, or if Cathy's hormones were playing a nasty trick, trying to give him a stroke.

9th April

Wednesday

Byron picked up her phone, curious to see who the stream of incoming WhatsApp messages were from. She'd put the phone in a locker during her morning workout, and now, as she towelled off, she realised there was something serious going down.

Cathy: *Hi girls, meet tonight for coffee & chat? x x*

Annabel: *Do you miss us already? Didn't get enough madness at the weekend?*

Cathy: *Yea, something like that. Need to talk...bring chocolate x x*

Annabel: *Everything ok hun?*

Cathy: *Get ur ass to Wicklow ASAP after work, no excuses x x*

Annabel: *Seriously Cathy, you have me worried now. I'm trying to ring, answer the phone!!!*

Becky: *What's up Sis? Where's the fire?*

Cathy: *Everything fine. Everyone fine. Kid's r fine. Just need to talk to my girls x x*

Becky: *Cud u not wait till after sunrise to start a texting frenzy. All the beeps woke me.*

Annabel: *Ha ha, Beck. Get your lazy ass out of bed. Half the day is gone.*

Becky: *No not half the day. I'm in nite mode now. Like a vampire, I do all my best work at nite.*

Cathy: *Kids will be asleep by 8. Need all here ASAP after that x x*

Annabel: *Ok, got the message. Will see u later. Only if I survive this day at work!!*

Becky: *Right Sis, do you need me to beat the crap outta Sam? Itching for a good brawl.*

Cathy: *Keep ur hands off Sam…but bring wine, u will need it.*

Annabel: *Feck sake, Cathy, will you answer your phone. I'm worried now. What's going on?*

Cathy: *Tonight @ 8 girls, see u then x x*

Byron scrolled through all the messages again, wondering, like the others, what was going on. She packed up her gym bag and headed for the carpark, thinking that she really didn't have time for another drama in her life. With her wedding only eight weeks away, she was already up to her eyes in it, stretched thin with appointments for meetings and decisions.

She threw her bag onto the passenger seat of her car and climbed in. Easing out of her parking space, she wished Cathy had saved her problem for another night – even next weekend, when there wouldn't be one hundred and one other things to worry about.

When she reached the office, she fired off a quick text to the group chat, letting them know she'd meet them all in Wicklow later.

"Morning, Byron," someone called from the kitchenette. "Coffee?"

"You bet," she called back. "Throw two of those little capsules in, will you? I think I'm going to need it to make it through the day."

***

Annabel hid the vibrating phone in her desk drawer, worried it might draw attention to her, but afraid to switch it off in case she missed something. Leaning back in her office chair, she took a moment to savour her strong black coffee. She realised coffee was the only thing keeping her going these days. An awful reality. It was high time she started eating healthier and looking after herself. She remembered how lovely it was spending the day with her mother on Sunday. Even though the woman drove her nuts, she vowed to make it a more regular commitment.

Maybe she could bring her mum out for lunch someday, or to the theatre, or even the cinema. Her mother would love that, and even though she still felt guilty, it soothed her to know she'd turned a corner.

"Excuse me, Annabel." The all too familiar and all too unpleasant voice pulled her from her thoughts. "If you could possibly find the time," Gemma, said, "I wonder if you could take a look at these files."

A large pile of thick folders dropped onto her desk, almost blocking out Gemma's sour face.

"What are they, Gemma?" Annabel asked, with more than a touch of irritation in her voice.

"Ms Connolly has requested a written report on each of these mismanaged fund cases. ASAP."

Gemma's nasal voice grated on Annabel's nerves. She gripped the edge of her desk and took a silent, calming breath. "Okay, but what are they, and what's it got to do with me?"

Gemma smirked and shook her head, as if speaking to an idiot. "Auditors have found discrepancies. They're looking for explanations as to why funds were moved or reallocated."

Annabel flicked through the first few folders. "Mismanaged funds?" She looked at Gemma, forcing herself not to scowl. "None of these clients are mine." She pushed them away. "These are nothing to do with me."

Gemma pushed the files back. "Well, they're old cases, belonging to reps who've left the company."

Annabel stared at her. There was something oddly familiar about the woman. Her scent? Maybe it was her shampoo or perfume – she couldn't put her finger on it, but if she found out, she'd be sure never to use it again. She raised an eyebrow, waiting for further explanation.

"Ms Connolly speaks so highly of you," Gemma said, enunciating each word, grinding on every last living nerve Annabel had. The side of her mouth lifted in a sneer. "Thinking of your experience and expertise, I suggested to Ms Connolly that you would be the perfect person to sort this mess out."

"Jesus, Gemma, are you kidding me?" Annabel jumped up from behind her desk to face her tormenter head on. "I'm not taking on someone else's shit." She gestured towards the stack of folders. "This is a bloody lawsuit waiting to happen, and I'm not putting my name anywhere near it. Forget it."

With a perfectly manicured hand, Gemma brushed some stray hairs from her suit jacket. She looked around the office, her eyes falling on the empty desk and coffee cup. "You have no choice, I'm afraid. Everyone else is busy. I'm working on a special project and you seem to be the only one sitting around, drinking coffee."

Annabel gasped as she listened to the other woman insult her. Since she'd started with the company two months ago, Gemma had made a name for herself among the staff. Party hard, and work less, seemed to be her motto. But not only that, she bullied and pushed others into doing unnecessary tasks, always managing to come out smelling of roses.

"Get real, Gemma," she snapped, furious to be spoken to like a child, and ready to make her point. "You have no idea what I do, or when I do It." She jabbed a finger at the other woman's face, closing the distance between them. "You're only with this company a wet week, and just because you have some sort of lesbian crush on the senior manager, it doesn't mean you run the place." She clamped her mouth shut, realising she'd gone too far. By speaking out loud about rumours of some sort of illicit office affair involving this woman and her manager, Annabel knew she's made a stupid mistake.

Gemma sniffed, her face flushing bright red. Then she turned on her heal and marched out of Annabel's office without another word.

"Shit, shit, shit," Annabel muttered, her eyes closed. *This is all I need.* With one last glance at the mountain of work she now possessed, she typed an email to Gemma, apologising for her dreadful behaviour, hoping the little bitch would not take the flippant remark about the lesbian affair straight to HR and get her fired.

***

Later that evening in Wicklow, after finally getting the children into bed, Cathy waited outside the sitting-room door to let Annabel finish her story uninterrupted.

"So now, I'm a sitting duck," Annabel said to Byron and Becky. "My heart almost stops every time the phone rings, wondering if it's the head of HR about to instigate disciplinary proceedings against me."

"Well, this Gemma sounds like a right little cow," Byron said, anger in her voice.

"She is. A sneaky little cow, actually. She's not there that long, but I never really took to her. A right brown-noser if I ever saw one, and I wasn't wrong when I said she wanted to lez it up with the senior manager. She'd do anything for a promotion. I shouldn't have said it out loud, though, to her face."

Nervous, Cathy entered the room, took a few squares of chocolate and a handful of popcorn out of Annabel's lap, then plonked herself into an armchair and waited for the questions to begin.

"Eh, hello," Becky said. "What's the story?"

"Yes," Byron added, "we've just heard all about Annabel's problems with the bi-sexual bully. I've given a rundown on where we are with the preparations needed to make my wedding the happiest day of my life, and we've also had to endure ten minutes of Becky battering on about incompetent stage crews, and venues designed to give you hepatitis C."

They all looked at Cathy. Fighting the urge to flee the room and lock herself in a cupboard, she glued herself to the chair and, facing her friends with a big smile, she threw her hands up in the air. "Guess what, guys? I'm pregnant."

Byron looked at Annabel, Annabel looked at Cathy, and Becky burst out laughing.

"Yeah, right, Sis, good one," Becky said, scooping up a handful of popcorn. "You're a few days late with the April Fool's gag, so now the joke is on you."

"Shut up, Becky," Byron said, looking at Cathy, her eyes narrowing as she studied her face. "She's serious."

She got up, crossed the room, and sat on the side of the chair, taking Cathy's hands in hers. "Cathy, love, are you all right? I mean, this is real, isn't it? It's not a joke?" She spoke gently, rubbing her friend's hands.

Moisture dammed in Cathy's eyes until it could hold no more, a tear sliding down each cheek. "No," she whispered, her head down, "it's not a joke. This is as real as it gets."

"Well, I guess that explains the sickness you had last week," Annabel, always the practical one, said.

Cathy nodded, but Annabel frowned. "Hang on, did you know about this last weekend?" She got to her feet. "Why were you out drinking and clubbing if you're pregnant? What's going on, Cathy? What are you playing at? Please tell me you didn't know."

Every word stung Cathy like a needle. She already felt the guilt. They would have to wait months for the scan, to see if the baby had been affected by her drunken state the previous weekend. However, she didn't like Annabel pointing it out, as if she hadn't already considered it.

"Of course I didn't know, Annabel," she said, trying to control her shaking body. "What do you take me for? A complete idiot?" She picked at the corner of a cushion, keeping her hands busy as she spoke to

94

her friends. "I found out yesterday, for certain, after a very anxious twenty-four-hour wait, several pregnancy tests, and a quick visit to my doctor yesterday morning."

As the looks of confusion and shock turned to concern on the girls' faces, Cathy relayed all the drama of the past week or so, explaining how she'd missed the signs, put the symptoms down to the school vomiting bug and stress, and that in thirty-four-and-a-half weeks, she would be a mammy again.

More coffee, chocolate, and popcorn were supplied while Cathy and her closest friends were brought back to earth at the realisation that soon there would be a brand new baby within the small group. Cathy's baby.

Becky fidgeted on the sofa, finally standing and pacing the room, obviously struggling with something on her mind.

She turned to Cathy, rubbing down the sides of her jeans. "So, Sis, I have to ask. Who's the father?"

Cathy gasped and glared at her sister, while Byron and Annabel sat silent, watching. "What? For fuck's sake, Becky, who do you think it is?" She waited a moment, taking in her sister's cocked eyebrow and questioning look.

"It's Sam, of course," she shouted. "Who the hell else would it be?"

Becky pulled back her shoulders, her eyes narrowing as she prepared to respond. "Don't jump down my throat. It's a reasonable question." She looked at the others, cocking her head and raising both eyebrows to encourage reaction.

Annabel coughed into her hand and sat up. "Actually, to be honest, Cathy, the thought crossed my mind as well."

Cathy couldn't believe this. First Sam had questioned her and now her closest friends were doubting her commitment and fidelity. Anger burned through her, the heat of her ire searing into her brain. She shot out of the chair and stomped towards Becky, who nearly fell back onto her seat in shock. "What do you think I am, some sort of Saturday-night slut? The goddam cheek of you!"

She turned to Annabel, shaking. "And you, do you think that as soon as I get the kids off to school, I have a quick *how's your father* with the postman, or the milkman, or any other type of man who happens to come knocking?"

Becky stepped in front of her, palms out in an obvious effort to placate her. "Ah, Cathy, we're not saying that. It's just, well, Sam has only been around a handful of times in the past while. This could hardly have been a planned decision, or are you trying to tell us that he sent you a turkey baster full of his best swimmers and you impregnated yourself?"

Byron and Annabel roared with disgust, while Cathy stood shaking her head and blinking. "Turkey baster, Becky? Jesus Christ, what's the matter with you?"

Annabel pulled Cathy to one side. "Come on, Cathy, sit down. Calm down." She led her back to the chair, sat her down, and knelt in front of her. "Now, tell us what happened. I presume this wasn't planned." She sent a warning look to Becky not to interfere.

Cathy took a sip of water, the glass shaking in her hands. "No, it wasn't planned. It's such a shock, I didn't even pick up on the obvious signs." She told them the baby was probably conceived around St Patrick's Day, according to the doctor, and that made sense. Sam had been home that weekend. The doctor confirmed that she was five weeks and four days pregnant and the baby was due in December, and the only mystery left to solve was why the pill she'd been taking had failed.

"So, girls," she said, trying to smile through the tears, "be warned – extra protection at all times, and twice on Sundays."

Becky edged closer, her shoulders slumped, head bowed. "I'm sorry, Sis. I didn't doubt you, not really. Of course Sam's the father. You know me with my gigantic mouth. I need to get a zip fitted. Your explanation makes much more sense than the turk—"

"Don't!" Cathy snapped. The room fell silent, everyone looking at her, as if expecting another blowout. Instead, she smiled, got up, and went to Becky, enveloping her in hug that said all was forgiven. "You, Becky, are going to an auntie again.

You're going to have a brand new little niece or nephew." She couldn't help smiling at the tears glistening in Becky's eyes.

"Promise me something, Becky," Cathy said with as much determination as she could manage.

Becky sniffled and raised a questioning eyebrow.

"Please don't wreck this one on me, too."

Becky wiped her eyes and cleared her throat, a big grin brightening her face up. "I'll try, I really will. But you know me, I can't promise anything."

"And please," Cathy said, looking at each of the three girls in turn, "not a word to anyone. I'm freaked out enough as it is without having to deal with questions from outfield."

"Mum's the word," Becky said, zipping her lip. Annabel nodded, a wistful smile spread across her face. Byron agreed not to mention a thing to anyone except Tom.

***

A strange feeling of dread washed over Bryon as she listened to Cathy and Annabel discuss pregnancy issues. She scrutinised Cathy's pale face. Clearly the girl was worried sick and had a tough road ahead, but why didn't she feel empathy for her? The only feeling she could identify within herself was annoyance that her wedding day would now be overshadowed with this pregnancy, and that she would no longer be the belle of the ball.

10th April

Thursday

Byron finished at the gym and took a short drive to a coffee shop. She ordered a mini-breakfast, with extra scrambled eggs and a full-fat latte.

"Feck it," she said, choosing a table by the window, "it's my day off. I deserve a treat."

Looking out onto the busy street, she people-watched the hustle and bustle of rush hour on this wet Thursday morning. Office workers strode passed, battling umbrellas, while parents guided young children draped in plastic coats towards the gate of the local primary school.

As she watched, her mind drifted to Cathy. She already thought of her as superwoman, but was surprised at how accepting her friend had been of the altered circumstances. This pregnancy was a life-changing event, designed to rock her world onto a completely new axis, mapping out an altogether different course than Cathy thought she was on.

She'd tried, last night, to lend her support, but beneath all the fake kind words and congratulations, she was furious. No matter what way she looked at it, going over and over it in her head, spinning it this way and that, she felt betrayed by her friend. She knew Cathy hadn't planned this on purpose to piss her off, but why, oh why, did it have to be now, just two months before her wedding? Cathy had the rest of her life to have babies, but this, please God, would be her one and only wedding day. She'd been planning it for two years, every little detail – not a stone was left unturned when it came to catering, flowers, cars, bands, or invitations.

When she'd seen Tom this morning, she'd told him exactly how she felt. "I know Cathy is my best friend, but, Jesus, a little bit of timing and discretion would have been nice."

Tom was exhausted, having just got home from the night shift as a fireman, and he had barely made it through the front door before Byron exploded in a mess of words and flaying hands.

"Byron, love," he'd said, taking hold of her wayward arms and holding them gently by her side. "What's the big deal? So Cathy is pregnant. So what? It's not like she hasn't been pregnant before. She already has two kids, right?"

"That's not the problem, Tom," she replied, sighing through her torment.

"Then what is it, pet?" he asked, glancing at the stairs, where Byron knew he wanted to drag his tired body.

Like a spoilt child, she screwed up her face and reluctantly voiced what had been going through her mind all night. "She is stealing my thunder, Tom."

"What does that even mean?" he asked, edging towards the stairs, but stopping when she released a loud sob. She took a deep breath to stifle the emotion bubbling into her throat and allowed Tom lead her to the second step.

"What do you mean, honey?" He knelt in front of her. "What has Cathy being pregnant got anything to do with you, or us?"

She explained with a shaky breath how she was feeling. Tom was the one person she hoped would understand and not judge her. "We're getting married in two months, Tom. This time should be all about us. You and me."

Tom rubbed his eyes and let out a deep sigh. "I'm sorry, honey, it's been a long shift and I'm almost asleep. What are you trying to say?"

Byron closed her eyes for a second and took a steadying breath. "Okay, well, I know it sounds selfish as hell, and I don't want to feel like this, but the truth is…I do. I want the next few weeks to be a whirl of bridal showers, with cute little cupcakes and floral arrangements, then going for dress fittings, and having last-minute single-friend lunches. It's all part of my wedding scenario."

She couldn't believe she was saying the words out loud. But she couldn't help how she was feeling. "I want to be the one everyone is talking about, Tom, wondering what dress I'll wear, even if I'll show up at all!"

Tom sat beside her and leaned his shoulder against hers. "For the first time in this relationship, Byron, I think I'm the sensible one."

She hiccupped as she laughed. "Before we get bogged down into married life, Tom, I wanted this wedding to be the best day of my life."

"I know, love, and it will be."

"It won't!" She sobbed into his shoulder. "I've been planning this day for two years, and now, just when I'm on the final straight, ready to shine in all my glory, Cathy swoops in and gives everyone something else to talk about."

"Byron, stop," he said, taking her hand and resting it on his heart. "Everyone knows that this wedding is the most important thing in your whole life. We've all being hearing about it for months now."

She shot him a look.

"And we don't mind," he added, without losing a beat, "because we all know that you're living for this one perfect day."

"Really?" She knew she'd wrecked a lot of heads with her constant talk about their wedding.

"Really. I know it. Your friends and family know it. Even the homeless man who camps outside the post office knows it. But the point is, I would never have tolerated this obsessive planning and organizing if I didn't think you deserved to have everything you wanted, and I want to give it to you. But just hold back a second, honey, and think about what you're saying here."

Bryon sniffed, letting Tom's soothing words bring her down. Tom, her constant voice of reason.

"You know Cathy didn't go out and deliberately 'steal your thunder'. She probably hasn't given our wedding a second thought since she found out about the baby." He rubbed her back, his hand strong and calming. "Talk to her, Byron. She'll understand where you're coming from. I bet she doesn't even realise you're upset? Does she?"

Bryon rested her head in her hands. "I know, you're probably right."

"And you know her situation is never going to take away from how incredibly hard you've worked to make our dream a reality, and how proud I'll be the day I see you walking down the aisle towards me, and you finally say 'I do'."

She smiled and laid her head on his shoulder again. "I can't wait to walk towards you, Tom. I can't wait to walk back down the aisle, clutching your hand." Her voice came out in a whisper, her mouth at his ear. "Our first journey as husband and wife."

"Yeah," he said, pulling her up with him, hugging her with arms of pure muscle. "So what if people are fussing over Cathy and her bump? At least it'll give me time to grab my new wife by the ass and give her a kiss she'll never forget."

"Ha, ha, you wouldn't dare? Not in front of your mother."

"Wanna bet?" He grinned, lust knocking the tiredness out of his eyes. He kissed her and led her upstairs. "I've already checked, we'll have time for a quickie after the church and before the photographs."

Byron laughed, unsure if he was serious or not.

"And again, after we greet our guests." He chuckled. "And then before the meal."

She licked her lips as he pushed her back on the bed and caressed her face with his nightshift stubble. If there was one thing she loved, it was his work face.

"And, perhaps, one more time after the cake," he said, moving down the bed and giving her a preview of the plans he'd made for their special day.

11th April

Friday

Sam packed his travel bag, readying himself for the trip back to London.

"I wish I didn't have to leave today," he said, throwing in socks and a bag of toiletries.

Cathy was sitting on the bed, watching him pack. "You've got to go, Sam." She leaned back on her elbows. "I'll be fine. You need to sort out all the crap that's going on with Sorcha and Aoife. They're playing you, big time."

She knelt up on the bed and rolled socks into a neat ball. "Anyway, we talked about this last night. I know you're not running out on me. I get it, but you need to deal with other things before you can make the move back to Ireland, fulltime."

Sam stopped packing and stepped over to the bed. He wanted her to believe what he had to say. "That's my intention, Cathy." He pulled her up to him and placed a hand on her still-flat belly. "I want to be here with you, building our life together, settling down and raising our family."

She smiled, her teeth gleaming in the soft light. "I want that, too."

"Last year was tough," he said, caressing her stomach, considering his words as he endeavoured to tie the future into the past. "Finding out about Sorcha, travelling over, getting to know her."

Cathy nodded, but remained silent.

"Despite the fact that Sorcha and her mother are trying to leech me for every penny I have, I think we're in a good place right now. She's happy knowing the truth about her family, and happy to know I'm around and willing to be part of her life." He slid his arms around Cathy's hips, pulling her closer. "She doesn't need me to be a fulltime parent – Aoife and Bill are doing that well enough. Me being there too much is actually confusing matters." He looked down at Cathy's belly again. "So this little nugget is probably a blessing in disguise, forcing me to make a decision – to make the break and move on with my life."

"In fairness," Cathy said, "you'd already come to that conclusion before we found out about the baby. And really, apart from tapping you for a few quid now and then, it looks like Sorcha's cool with just knowing you haven't forgotten her. Even if you're not with her every day."

He leaned in, nuzzling her neck, letting her sweet scent wash over him. "It'll just be for a few days, to tie up loose ends." He kissed the pulsing beat above her collarbone. "I'll be back to take care of you, before you have time to miss me."

Cathy pulled his head up and found his mouth. He sucked on her tongue as she deepened the kiss, then let her push him back on the unmade bed. She straddled him, her knees on both sides of his hips, her bottom pressing into him as she bit his lip.

Sam, bone-hard now, got his two hands between their bodies, unbuttoning her blouse, while Cathy raked her fingers through his hair, her mouth drinking him in.

Coming up for air, she removed her blouse, unhooked her bra, and offered her breasts to him. "You can look after me now," she rasped, her breath heavy, guiding his mouth to her erect nipple, groaning when he teased it with his teeth and tongue.

"I adore your tits," Sam said. "I think they're getting bigger." He sucked on her other nipple, her soft flesh pressing into his mouth. "Jesus, I'm rock hard just feeling them here, smothering my face."

"Oh, God," she moaned, grabbing the back of his head and pulling him against her. As he sucked, she ground herself into him, again and again, her motions nearly bringing him to the brink.

He grabbed her by the hips, spun her around, and lifted her skirt in one quick movement. Once he dropped his trousers, he knelt and came close up behind her, pulling aside the flimsy scrap of material covering her soaking glory.

Kissing her beautiful back, he guided himself against her, slipping his tip between her lips, her wet heat spreading into his balls and straight up to his head. With one steadying hand on her hip, while the other caressed her swollen breast, he eased forward and entered her in a long, slick movement of absolute pleasure. Whimpers escaped from Cathy's lips as he filled her to the hilt, then pulled back, inch by slow inch, to start again.

Jesus, don't pull out," she said, panting as she looked back over her shoulder.

He smiled and leaned over her, licking her hot skin. Then, holding her tight, he moved in and out, slow to begin with, working with her reciprocal movements as she curved her back and pressed into him. They worked together, urging each other on, moaning and groaning as they built up a frenzied rhythm, Sam filling and stretching Cathy with every stroke, every cry, and every touch, their mutual pleasure magnified by their shared desire to reach new heights of love and passion.

When she reached down and cupped his balls, sparks exploded inside his head. The heat of her hand as she squeezed on his soft flesh caught his breath, and he cried out her name in the sweet explosive release of a mind-blowing orgasm, his boiling seed pouring into her, her scream of ecstasy driving him to a new height as she rose up, her pussy clamping around him, both of them quivering as she milked every drop of cum he had.

Wet and exhausted, she flopped sideways on the bed, her chest heaving, eyes closed. Sam covered her with his sweaty body, his own chest working overtime as he attempted to get air back into his lungs.

"I think I might have passed out there for a second," he said, once he could speak again.

She struggled under his limp body. "I can't breathe!"

"Oh, shit, sorry." He rolled onto his side, bringing her with him into a spooning position. "Sorry, are you all right?" He ran his hands over her wet skin.

"Wow, where the hell did that come from?" she asked, threading her fingers up along his hip. "That was so intense. Seriously, I thought my feet were going to fall off.

"Don't know," he said, closing his eyes and breathing deep. He needed to slow his heartbeat.

She turned to face him, her warm hand caressing his bottom. "It must be the pregnancy hormones."

Sam cranked one eye open just enough to see her. "Well, if that's what I have to look forward to for the next eight months, you'll hear no complaints from me." Her hand had him growing hard again. He shifted forward to rub against her leg.

"Again?" she asked, an eyebrow raised, her bright smile showing she was well up for it.

He eased her onto her back and spread her legs, inching his way down the bed. "Again," he whispered, kissing and licking her stomach as he trailed his hand across her mound.

"Oh, God," she gasped, pushing against him, running her fingers through his hair.

Sam kissed the sensitive skin on her inner thigh, his fingers soaked as he circled her core.

"Don't worry, Cathy, I'm just going to say hello to Baby, using the most direct route."

She groaned and bucked, leaving him wondering just how much more he could love this woman giving herself so freely to him. With every fibre of his being he promised to protect and care for this world they had created, hoping to never see the dark side of betrayal again.

12th April

Saturday

Sam flew back to London, intent on clearing his head and sorting out his life. Travelling back and forth was exhausting, and not what he wanted for the future. He'd arranged to pick up Sorcha early, needing to speak properly with her, to explain all that was going on. He wanted her to know where his mind was at and endeavour to find a middle ground, something that would suit them both going into the future.

With the car parked outside her house, he made his way towards the gate. The front door was flung open and Sorcha ran out, her face contorted with anger as she stomped past him.

"Sorcha," he called, trying to catch her as she passed. "What's going on?" She shrugged him off, eyes blazing in silent warning, and continued out of the garden and down the road.

Aoife appeared at the front door, checked to see which way her daughter had gone, then turned to Sam.

"What's going on, Aoife?" he asked, positive he'd walked into the middle of something he wasn't sure he wanted to be involved in. She gestured for him to go inside, away from prying eyes. "What's happened to make her bolt out like that?"

Aoife went through and started to clear breakfast dishes into the sink, gesturing for Sam to sit at the kitchen island. She sighed and shook her head.

"As usual, Sorcha has a bee up her arse about not getting her own way. Believe me, Sam, this is not the first temper tantrum she's thrown, and it certainly won't be the last."

Sam rolled his eyes and nodded, trying to show that he understood all about girls and their tempers. "What's it all about this time?" He got up and helped Aoife clear some dishes.

She flicked the switch on the kettle, then leaned against the kitchen counter. "She wants to go to a concert with her friends. I'm not letting her go." She pursed her lips, exhaling through her nose, her frustration patent. "She's ten years old, for Christ's sake. She can't go to a concert on her own."

Sam considered this. Conscious he'd be back in Ireland soon, he reckoned he should grasp this opportunity to reassure Sorcha of his commitment and try to earn a few well-needed brownie points. He watched Aoife make the coffee.

"Maybe there's a way I can help out." Uncomfortable talking about such things with her, he nevertheless pushed on. "If it's because you can't afford to let her go, then maybe I could help out there."

Aoife's face flushed red and she turned away. "It's not that." She looked up at the ceiling, her expression pained. "Well, that's part of the problem, but I do think she's too young to be going to this thing on her own. There's no way I can afford to buy tickets for her, or to go with her, so…no, she can't go. She'll just have to learn the meaning of the word no."

Sam tried a different approach. "Maybe I can bring her. Would that be okay?" He waited for a response, but Aoife didn't look around. "I'll pay for the tickets and whatever else is needed. It would actually help me out if you'd let me."

She looked at him, her brows creased in a questioning frown. "How's that?" She placed a cup of coffee in front of him.

"Well, there's something I need to speak to you and Sorcha about," he said, looking towards the front door, then back again, "but now I'm wondering if it's such a good idea."

"What is it, Sam?" she asked, fidgeting with her own steaming mug.

He cleared his throat and decided to just get it over with. Better to have Aoife's reaction to his news first, before he broke it to Sorcha. He told her about his relationship with Cathy and how they'd recently discovered that she was pregnant, and that he'd decided to move back to Ireland. "I've been thinking about it for a while, moving back, I mean, even before this baby news hit, but now, I suppose the decision has been made for me, and it's as good a time as any."

Aoife opened the back door, lit a cigarette and took a deep drag. "How do you feel about all this baby stuff, then?" she asked, blowing out a stream of white smoke.

Sam couldn't help smiling. "Getting used to the idea now. I wasn't afforded the opportunity to

113

know about Sorcha or be a parent to her, so it's all pretty new to me."

Aoife smoked in silence. Sam sipped his coffee and thought about the days, months, and years ahead.

"You know, I'd no intention of ever contesting your adoption of Sorcha," he said, keeping his voice quiet, wanting to reassure her.

She closed the back door and placed her cup beside the sink. "When you first turned up, I was terrified. I fought tooth and nail to protect what I had, trying to stop you getting anywhere near our family." Her eyes softened and she unclasped her hands. "Sam, the more time you spent with Sorcha, with all of us, made me realise you just wanted to be part of your daughter's life. You didn't want to take her away from us." Her voice broke and she coughed to clear her throat. "She's my baby girl, Sam. I simply couldn't let you take her away."

He reached out and took her hand. "I'm sorry, Aoife. None of this has been easy. Last September, when Sinead confessed to having our baby and leaving her with you, a million and one thoughts raced through my head." He nodded to himself as he thought back. "I wondered if she looked like me. Was she tall? Was she happy at school? Clever, mischievous, caring and kind? All the aspects of me I'd hope a child of mine would inherit."

His smile tightened. Sorcha was nothing like him. She'd somehow managed to be born with her mother's less than admirable attributes. He pushed the horrible realisation out of his eyes. It wasn't fair on Aoife to see that. "But never once did I ever think about taking her away from you. I needed to meet her, Aoife, to get to know her. Looking back, it was a selfish thing to do – I should have waited until she was a bit older, or I was a little less shell-shocked. But the fact remains that, through no fault of my own, I've missed out on the nine years of her life, and I wanted to make up for that, in any small way I could, more than happy to be the satellite dad." He shrugged and swallowed the emotion back. "I just needed to know my own flesh and blood, and…for her to know that I exist.

"Now that I know she's safe and well cared for," he continued, "I'm good with you and Bill being the only parents she requires. You certainly don't need me sticking my oar in at this stage. You're doing a fantastic job, Aoife. Sorcha is a credit to you both." He didn't mind spinning the white lie to make her feel better. "I'm moving back to Ireland, but I'll always be around for Sorcha, whenever she might need me. I'll make sure she understands that."

He looked straight into Aoife's eyes, willing her to understand. "I know this won't be a 'traditional happy family', but I'll still be part of her life, for as long as she wants me to be." He broke off a piece of biscuit and dunked it in his cooled coffee, needing to do something with his hands.

Aoife brushed something off her sleeve and took his cup away. "I'm pretty sure she'll appreciate that, Sam."

"I know treating Sorcha to this concert might look like I'm trying to buy her affection, but, really, that's not the case. It's my way of saying goodbye and taking a step back from her everyday life."

He watched as she rinsed their cups and stacked them into the dishwasher. Would she understand? There wasn't really anything to agree on – he'd made his decision, but it would be better to have her blessing. Just as she turned to speak, the front door opened and slammed shut. They both looked towards the hallway, and it didn't take long before Sorcha appeared in the kitchen doorway, her eyes red, face flushed.

"Jesus, Sorcha," Aoife said, stepping forward with her arms out, but stopping at her daughter's stiffened posture.

Sam felt awkward and decided to remain seated. No point adding to her sense of being threatened. She would run again, he was sure of it. He needed to speak to her, to get this all sorted.

Sorcha looked from Sam to Aoife, and back again. A look of defiance scorched her face as she raised an eyebrow, daring anyone to piss her off again.

Sam shifted straighter in his chair. "Aoife, would it be okay if I explained to Sorcha what we agreed?"

Aoife clenched a tea-towel between her hands, twisting it into a tight knot. "Go ahead, Sam, I think she would be happier hearing it from you, anyway.

I'm not so sure she will listen to anything I have to say."

Sorcha, arms crossed and chin raised, waited. When Sam didn't speak, she scowled and tapped her foot. "Well, what's the big surprise? Am I getting a new dolly, or a big teddy bear from Uncle Sam?"

For a second, Sam considered taking back his offer and teaching the girl some manners, but guilt crept in when he remembered the baby news that had to be broached.

"Your mother and I have been talking—"

"Oh, did she tell you all about it then? How I'm going to be 'Billy no mates' in school, coz I'm the only one not allowed to go to the Little Mix concert?"

"Now, wait just one second," Aoife cut in. "You know it's not as simple as that. It's an expensive trip, and we have bills and a mortgage to look after—"

"Yeah, yeah, I've heard it all before," Sorcha said, plonking herself on the nearest chair, big fat tears and sobs rattling her body, almost as if an invisible switch had been activated.

Sam couldn't stand it any longer. When he received a nod of approval from Aoife, he faced his daughter, intent on getting through this as fast as he could, though he wasn't sure he had what it took to penetrate an obviously heartbroken child.

"Sorcha, I'm going to bring you to the concert. My treat."

The tears stopped. The face straightened. Sorcha looked at him. "Just you and me?"

"Yes, and your friends, of course. I want this to be one of the best memories you have of me, not as a father, but as a friend." The last bit sounded far too corny, even to his ears, but he carried on.

"I want us to be able to spend this time together, because, well…" He paused, trying to find the right words.

"What is it, Sam? Are you dying?"

"What? No." He smiled, wondering where kids got their dramatic flair from. Had he been like that? If he had, he couldn't remember. "Look, Sorcha, I'm moving back to Ireland."

"You're going back?" Her voice was so quiet, Sam had to watch her mouth to make out the words. "Why?"

He figured honesty was the best policy, like ripping off a Band-Aid, so he took a deep breath and let it out. "The woman I love, Cathy is her name, is pregnant. She's going to have my baby." He let that settle for a moment before continuing. "It doesn't change how I feel about you. You're still my daughter, but it means I won't be living here in London anymore. I need to go home, Sorcha."

Given her current emotional state, he expected tears, or shouting, or at the very least a stomp of her foot, but all he got was silence, with the odd blink thrown in.

"I won't be far away," he said, "just across the water – a plane ride away, less than an hour really, once you're up in the air."

Sorcha remained silent, causing Sam to wonder if she understood what was happening, or was she feeling instant abandonment at the news.

"Once I'm settled again, you know, in a week or two, you can come and visit."

"Okay," she said.

"Really?" He smiled, relieved at the positive reaction, even if it was just one word. "You're not upset then, about me moving back?"

"No, Sam, I'm not upset," she answered, her voice sweet and kind, acceptance spilling out of her. "I'm not upset, because you're going to be a real dad. That is so awesome. I'm happy for you." She flung her arms around his neck.

"Really?" he asked, not a little surprised she was taking the news so well.

"Yes, really, Sam. Look, I know you're my biological dad, but as far as I'm concerned, you're not my real dad. My dad, Bill, is. And Mum is my real mum, no matter what it says on my birth certificate, or adoption certificate, or any other type of certificate."

Aoife came forward to pull Sorcha from Sam's arms, hugging her to herself.

"I love them both, more than words can say," Sorcha said, looking back over her shoulder at Sam. She turned back to Aoife. "I know I'm a right bitch sometimes, mum, but if I had to choose any parents in the world, you and dad would be the ones I'd pick."

With her arms still wrapped tight around her mother's waist, Sorcha turned to Sam again. "I'm happy for you. You're going to be a brilliant dad. Don't worry about me, I already have a brilliant mum and dad, so you need to go and share your brilliance with someone else."

Sam blinked back welling tears on witnessing her loving, meaningful words towards her mother, and him. It certainly altered his opinion of the spoilt brat he'd wanted to throttle five minutes ago. This was a girl he was now proud to call his daughter.

"Sorcha," he said, reaching out to hold her hand, "I am so relieved. I'll always be here for you, no matter what. You know that, right? Good or bad, early morning or late at night, I'm here, on the end of the phone, ready and willing to take your call."

"I know, Sam, and I'll come and visit. Maybe on school holidays or long weekends, or something. I'd love to see my Irish granny and grandad again." She turned to Aoife. "They're cool."

Sam couldn't believe the maturity she was showing. This time he let the tears flow, his heart bursting with pride. "Anytime you want, Sorcha.

You're always welcome. The door will be open for you, no matter what."

She let go of Aoife and threw herself into his arms. "I love you, Sam." She squeezed him and kissed his ear. "We're going to have so much fun in Ibiza."

Still on cloud nine, it took seconds for the words to sink in. Sam flicked a look at Aoife. "Ibiza? What has Ibiza got to do with anything?"

Sorcha leaned back and looked under her eyelashes at him, her smile so sickly sweet it was nearly dripping sugar. "That's where the concert is on. The English dates are sold out and Ibiza is the last date on their tour this year." Her eyes widened, almost as big as her smile.

"Wait? No, hang on a minute." He tried to untangle himself out of Sorcha's firm grasp.

"Sorcha, you're a very lucky girl," Aoife said. "A trip to Ibiza, a new baby, and all on the same day?"

Sam caught the look in Aoife's eyes. "Ibiza. Right." He said it more to himself than the others, full sure he'd just been played, bigtime.

13th April

Sunday

After taking her mother out for lunch, Annabel decided to head to Wicklow to help keep Cathy's children amused for a few hours, lending Cathy the chance to have a well-deserved rest.

If the truth be told, she was looking for any reason not to go home. She didn't want to be on her own. Jean Luc was away in Abu Dhabi, and would be for another few weeks. While she spoke to him every few days via Skype, she still missed his suave and borderline-arrogant ways.

She'd taken her time with him, knowing there was a different man beneath the arrogant exterior. By chipping away at the French façade, she'd got to know the real man, someone she would love to one day be an important part of her life.

It was well known that European men, be it French, German, Spanish, or Italian, had a more sophisticated, worldly way about them. She believed it was the way they were raised. Jean Luc was certainly well-travelled, and extremely well-read, and she could see how people viewed him as a know-all bigshot, compared to the more timid, laidback Irish man. Despite the initial persona he exuded, Annabel loved how he wasn't afraid to show immense affection, whether it be in their lovemaking, or in the company of friends and work colleagues. It was his confidence and easy charm that attracted her and, so far, no-one had been able to resist it.

Even Byron's tough, macho, fireman fiancé welcomed him with open arms, meeting him for pints or a bit of pub grub a couple of times. Jean Luc held himself well in any social situation, and his easy, loving nature magically drew Annabel deeper into their relationship. She realised that she missed him more than she'd expected. Earlier on in their relationship, she'd enjoyed his company, but on a casual basis. Now things had developed into something deeper, possibly long-term.

She couldn't deny that she was lonely without him, craving their intimate nights together, making love, sharing thoughts and dreams, getting to know one another, as lovers do. What she wouldn't give to curl up on the sofa, snuggle into his side, and feel the strong beat of his steady heart beneath his well-chiselled chest. She wished for his arms to wrap around her, securing her by his side while he whispered sweet nothings in her ear. "Everything is going to be okay," he would say, brushing wisps of hair from her eyes, protecting her from the dark thoughts of insecurity that swarmed through her mind.

Taking a deep breath, she tried to shake the sense of panic threatening to engulf her if she didn't calm herself. Her chest and throat tightened so much she gasped for breath, buzzing her window down to let some air in. No way could she drive in this state. She pulled the car to the side of the road and hit the hazard lights with a shaking hand, looking around to make sure she was out of the line of traffic. Cold sweat beaded on her neck and forehead as her arms and legs prickled with goose bumps.

Each breath came fast and shallow, the sweat now running down her face and back, her lungs screaming out as she gripped the steering wheel with both hands, her knuckles whitened. She needed to hold on to something, to focus, to slow her breathing and stop her heart from exploding out of her chest.

It had to be a panic attack. *How in the fuck am I having a panic attack?* What if she had a heart attack on the side of the road? Who would help her? She slammed the steering wheel and rooted in her bag for her phone, nearly emptying everything out before locating it. With shaky finger and blurred vision, she googled *panic attack* and tried to focus on the words swimming before her eyes, hoping there was some miracle cure available to her right here, right now, before she died in her car on the side of the road, alone.

Slow your breathing, one site advised, while another said that the feeling of imminent death was normal, and it was best to control your breathing to help relax your body. Once that happened, the panic would soon pass.

Having no option but to trust Google, she brought all her focus back to her breathing. She chanted out a mantra, hoping it would distract her from the impending heart attack and help feed her lungs with steady breaths of air.

"Breath in, one, two, three," she said, closing her eyes. "Breath out, one, two, three."

By round ten, things felt marginally better. She couldn't care less what she looked like to passers-by. The pounding in her chest had eased and her hands relaxed their death grip on the steering wheel. Her shoulders slumped forward as she continued with her chant, filling her lungs on each inhalation.

"Breath in, one, two, three," pause, "breath out, one, two, three."

After a while she was able to open her eyes with a degree of certainty she wouldn't faint. She pulled her phone closer on the passenger seat and calculated the time-difference between Ireland and the Emirates. "Ten p.m. in Abu Dhabi," she said, speed-dialling Jean Luc's number, needing to hear his voice.

"I miss you, Jean Luc," she said in a rush when he answered with a polite hello.

"Mon, petit reine, I am missing you, too. I am in a lonesome place while you are not at my side."

"I needed to hear your voice, Jean Luc," she whispered, afraid he could hear the panic still evident in her words. "I need to see you."

"I will be with you again soon, my sweet. Bientot, ma Cherie, bientot.

Annabel's body relaxed as she let his words flow over her. "I think I'm falling in love with you, Jean Luc," she said before she even knew she was saying it. Releasing those words eased her heart considerably.

"Well, my sweetness, it is not before your time that you finally agree to this." His voice was so soft in her ear. "I have loved you forever, but did not need to scare you. I am wonderful that you feel the same way also. My love for you is everything, please believe that."

Relief washed over her in a cleansing wave. "I believe, Jean Luc. Please come home to me soon. I want to see your face, touch your body, and feel you here with me, beside me."

"In six short days I will be with you, my Annabel. I will kiss you, and touch you, and love you until you scream in pleasure. I will say the words, I love you, out loud for everyone to hear."

Her heart raced and her breath quickened, but this time not from panic – from Jean Luc's words hitting the spot.

"I'm here," she whispered, "waiting for you. Please keep safe and be home to me soon."

"Only six more nights to sleep, Mon Cherrie, and I will have you wrapped in my arms. Will you wait for me?"

"Yes, Jean Luc, yes, I'll be counting the days." She realised this conversation had turned into something from a Mills & Boon novel – romance and mush, and declarations of undying love. She couldn't hold back the laugh that escaped her, feeling like a fool, but lots better than she had in weeks.

"What is the joke, ma petit?"

"Oh, nothing really," she said, thinking for a moment how good it was between them. "Do you know something, Jean Luc? You bring out the best in me, always, and I love you for that."

"Oui, love is what the feeling is that is happening between us. We are good as two people, no? We will be better when we are together again. Dynamite!"

Though his wording sometimes confused her, she was happy enough to get the general sentiment. She said goodbye and ended the call. Feeling calm enough to continue her journey, she dabbed the sweat off her face and neck and started the car, then pulled back out onto the road. She wouldn't let anyone hurt her. It wasn't an option now to be weak and scared. She was in love with the most wonderful man, and he loved her back. What more was required? She could climb Mount Everest, swim the seven seas, even conquer her feelings of anxiety, sure in the knowledge that no matter what anyone else thought of her, she had the love of a very special man. That was more than enough. She turned up the radio and buzzed down the window, letting the wind whip through her hair as she powered down the road towards Wicklow and her best friend.

14th April

Monday

"Annabel Clancy," she said, answering the phone.

"Annabel, what's the ETA on those files I gave you last week?" Gemma's shrill voice cut into her head, but considering the fine line she was already walking, she tried her best to be courteous and polite.

"Gemma, lovely to hear from you. The reviews are coming on slowly. I've written the preliminary reports on most cases, so I'm hoping to have the rest finished by Wednesday. That should—"

"Wednesday?" Gemma snapped. "That's not good enough. I don't think you understand the seriousness of this situation, Annabel. Ms Connolly expects those particular cases to be top priority. She wants the reports ASAP! Wednesday is not acceptable."

Annabel nearly growled, her anger rising. She gritted her teeth, determined to stand up to this bully. "Now hold on a minute, Gemma. Who the hell do you think you are? You're not my superior, and you have absolutely no authority to tell me what is or isn't acceptable. I won't—"

"You're right, of course, Ms Clancy," Gemma cut in, "I'm not your superior, but I am the one who will be pointing out, with great detail, your incompetency to Ms Connolly if those reports are not finished."

"What? What's going on here? You can't—"

"Oh, I can," Gemma said, jumping in again. "I've been keeping an eye on you. Even the great Annabel Clancy is not squeaky clean."

Annabel couldn't believe what she was hearing. "What are you talking about?" She wished she could tell this woman to fuck off.

"I've been doing a little digging around," Gemma answered, her words and tone heavy with distain. "Some extracurricular investigations, if you like. Seems all is not as it should be, especially with a number of your clients."

Annabel was gobsmacked. *Extracurricular investigations? What is this woman on about?*

"Complaints have been made, Annabel, by both clients and members of staff. Funds are being redirected for no apparent reason, and stock is losing value or being mismanaged. There was also one very serious complaint involving an elderly investor who said you made advances towards him in return for a lucrative business deal."

Air rushed out of Annabel's lungs, leaving her speechless. This was the first she'd heard of any complaints being made against her, ever. No way was this crap true. Gemma had to be fabricating some sort of hate campaign against her, but she still felt sick at the nature of the complaints the bitch had invented.

The woman's scurrilous accusations had to be challenged, but there was no point losing her rag. Not yet. She took a steadying breath. "I don't know what kind of game you're playing here, Gemma. You and I both know that everything you just said is completely untrue. In fact, those are some very serious allegations you've come out with there. Where's your evidence?"

Gemma snorted. "Evidence? I don't need evidence, as I am not directly involved, but rumour has it there is an ongoing internal investigation looking into the issue. Your ID number has been flagged with the auditors, and notes are being kept. I'd thread carefully if I were you, Ms Clancy, it would seem to me that you are on borrowed time here."

Annabel glared at the phone and fought back the urge to smash it off the wall. "That's all bullshit and you know it, Gemma. That internal investigation has nothing to do with me, or my work. Whatever scheming psycho game you're playing here is way out of line, and I'll be making a complaint myself to the Human Resources department on your behaviour and unacceptable threats against me."

Gemma laughed. "Oh, you're going to HR, are you? Well, when you do, would you ask them to give me a call? I have a nice little voice recording here on my mobile phone of you making derogatory remarks regarding me and the sexual orientation of your senior manager, Ms Connolly. It is without doubt that I've been traumatised since the attack on me, and feel so fragile as a result of being bullied by a so-called colleague on the grounds of my sexual preferences. That is, in my opinion, grounds for instant dismissal of the offender. You. I can, and I will, provide evidence to verify my claim, and have no problem testifying in a court of law to that effect."

Wild horses couldn't hold Annabel back from wanting to rip this woman's head straight off. Jesus, one flippant slip of the tongue and this crazy bitch wanted to get her fired for sexual harassment. Even more distressing was that Gemma had recorded their conversation. *What's that about? Why does this woman hate me so much?* They'd barely met, didn't actually know each other, and apart from a personality clash, there was no reason she could see to be despised so much the crazy woman wanted to get her fired.

She squeezed the phone, then took a deep, calming breath. "Gemma, please forgive what I said last week. It was a slip of the tongue. I was tired and hungry and you had just dumped a ton of extra work on my desk. I really didn't mean anything nasty by it, and if you took offence, then I am truly sorry and I apologise."

"Apology not accepted, Annabel," Gemma snarled. "I don't like you. You're a stuck-up bitch who thinks she can waltz around here like a queen bee. No one else gets a look in while you're around, do they? No one gets one ounce of notice."

"Gemma, I don't try to—"

"Perhaps I can learn to like you, Annabel, but you see, at the moment I feel under so much pressure, I'm not sure when something might slip out and I might accidently tell someone about the bullying and harassment."

131

Annabel remained silent, shocked by the woman's gall. She had the recording, and she was willing to use it.

"I'm sure if you were able to get those files done by, say, tomorrow morning, I would feel a whole lot better, and I'd be more inclined to keep my mouth shut."

It didn't require being a rocket scientist for Annabel to work out she was being blackmailed by a manipulative, sadistic bitch. But what could she do? If she refused to bend, she'd have to face a disciplinary meeting and maybe lose her job. The only option she had was to agree to the woman's unreasonable demands.

"Fine," she bit out, "I'll have the reports first thing tomorrow. Nine o'clock okay? Or do you want them faxed in by seven?"

"No need for the attitude," Gemma said. "Nine a.m. is fine. Get your work done and up to standard, Annabel, and we won't have a problem."

Annabel stared straight ahead as the phone went dead. *Thank God that's over.* She shook her head and ran a hand over her sweaty forehead. If there was any chance of her getting this work done, she'd be working all night. She looked at the clock on the wall. "Well, I can kiss that hot relaxing bubble bath goodbye."

15th April

Tuesday

Cathy scrambled to answer the house phone. "Hello," she said, waiting to see who it was.

"Cathy? It's Gary, are you all right? You sound out of breath."

She cringed, not wanting him to know about the baby yet, or that she'd spent the past half hour vomiting over the toilet bowl without the children noticing.

"I'm fine, Gary, I just ran to get the phone, that's all. What do you want?" She wasn't in the mood for excuses or sob stories today.

"I'm ringing to tell you, actually, that I have a bit of time off, tonight, tomorrow, and Thursday. I was going to offer to take the children, but if it's too much trouble for you to be civil to me, well then forget it. I won't bother."

Cathy fumed. She really didn't need this now, but knew if she called his bluff, they'd end up in a huge fight, the children wouldn't get to see their dad, and he would find a way of making that her fault.

She bit her tongue. "Look, Gary, I've a lot on my mind so, yes, of course the children would love to see you. In fact, they ask every day when you'll be taking them again." That dig had her smiling.

"Right, well, I'll come down later to collect them. What time suits?"

"After dinner is grand, but make sure you go shopping. I don't want a repeat of the cookies for breakfast and melon balls for lunch, like you gave them last time."

"Ah, Jesus, that was one fucking time. Stop acting like you're sending your children to an irresponsible teenager. I'm their dad. I'm just as capable of looking after them as you are."

"When it suits you," she said, getting another dig in. It wasn't often she got one over on him, never mind two.

He groaned. "Look, I'm not getting into this again. If you don't want me near my own children, then go and get a restraining order against me. Tell your sob story to the judge and see if he thinks giving my own children healthy fruit and a treat is grounds for stopping me seeing them."

Knowing he was right didn't make it any easier for her to accept how unreasonable she was being.

"Oh, I forgot," he said, chuckling, "you can't do that, can you? And do you know why? Let me tell you, you don't have a leg to stand on and you know it."

She hated being wrong, and it ground her nerves when she was wrong when Gary was right. Despite him being lax with maintenance, he adored his children. He was a great dad to them, and would never put them in harm's way. Okay, maybe they ate cookies for breakfast sometimes, and on the odd occasion they didn't brush their teeth, but she knew they were safe and looked after and, most importantly, loved. She had no choice but to back down and accept defeat on this one.

"All right, look, I'm sorry," she said, "I'm just tired and cranky."

"Well, go take a tablet." His voice held no sympathy. "Don't take your bad mood out on me, right?"

Cathy bit down on her lip, forcing herself to keep silent before she said something she might regret. Instead, she decided to try the *let's end this conversation and get him off the phone* option.

"Call down after six. I'll have them fed and ready to go." She wondered if it was wise to speak her mind, or just shut up and keep the peace. This concerned her children, and when it came to them, she fought tooth and nail. She didn't give a hoot who she pissed off. "Gary, can you at least promise me one thing?"

He sighed. "What?"

"Please don't ring me later and tell me you have to cancel. If I tell the children you're coming, it's not fair on them when you postpone. It breaks my heart to see their disappointment. I hate doing it to them."

"I won't cancel on them," he said after a long pause. "Millie and Jack are staying with me until Thursday. You can go ahead and tell them that. Tell

135

them to think of the games they want to play, and the dinners they want while they're here. I can't offer better than that, now, can I?"

He sounded like he meant every word of it, so she had no option but to trust he wouldn't let them down this time. "Right, well, I'll see you later," she said. "After six, all right?"

"Okay, and Cathy...?" There came a discernible pause. "Thanks."

She didn't know how to react to that. The last thing she expected from her ex was for him to extend any kind of olive branch. "For what?" she asked, more to give him the opportunity to explain.

"Ah, for being so understanding, in the past, and over the last few weeks. I'm trying my best, Cathy. I'm turning my life around, getting it back on track."

She caught her breath, unable to help herself, confused that she was actually sympathising with her ex-husband. When had she started to care about him and all his problems? Must be the bloody pregnancy hormones making her soft in the head.

Eager to get off the phone before she started declaring her undying love for the rat bastard, she shook her head and told him not to be late, putting her firmly back in the nagging ex-wife category she felt so comfortable in.

***

Gary sat back in his chair, intent on planning the next few days with the children, when his phone rang.

"Yo, Bud," a man said, his voice gritty and as Dublin as you'd get.

"All right, Anto?" Gary responded, wishing he'd checked the caller's identity first.

"Yeah, Bud, just giving you a heads-up for a dog on the track tonight. Racing at Shelbourne Park. Could be a tidy sum in it if you play your cards right."

"Yeah? Sounds good, but you know, Bud, I'm already up to me neck in it." He pushed back the voice in his head telling him not to turn down the chance to make a few quid.

"It's pretty much a sure thing, Gaz," Anto said. "Put a ton on the each-way forecast. You know the drill."

Gary grimaced. He'd be gambling with money he didn't have. If he was to put on the bet, he'd have to borrow the stake. His mind raced. *Is it a chance worth taking?* It was tempting, he knew that, but there was never, ever a sure thing when it came to dog racing. But all that logic went out the window as he imagined the profit he could make in such a short time tonight. It got his pulse racing, calculating the odds on each forecast bet. Then he remembered something.

"Ah, Jesus, Anto, I've just remembered, I've got my kids staying with me tonight. I can't make it, sorry."

A frosty silence hung in the air, and Gary wondered if the call had been disconnected.

"I don't think you fully understand me here, Bud," Anto finally said, his tone no longer friendly. "You owe me a grand, and I want it back. Simple. I'm giving you a sure thing. Race is all but fixed." His threatening tone sent a chill through Gary. "Find the money, bet on the dogs, keep the spoils, and pay me back my fucking money. Comprendo?"

Gary squeezed his eyes shut. *Shit, this could turn nasty if I don't calm the mad fucker down.* "Look, be reasonable, Anto, I've got my kids tonight and—"

"I don't care if the fucking President of the United States of America is fuelling up Air Force One and flying across the Atlantic to visit you in your shitty little flat, my friend. You just get yourself into town and meet me at the track. Nine o'clock, right?"

Gary remained quiet, knowing Anto wasn't finished with him yet.

"And if I don't see that pretty-boy face of yours tonight, Bud, consider it rearranged at a future date. How would a cocktail of broken nose and matching black eyes suit you?" Gary had to hold the phone away as Anto coughed and spluttered into his ear. His stomach turned when he heard him hack up and spit out what sounded like half his lung.

"Are you there?" Anto asked.

"Yeah, Anto, I'm here."

"Just make sure you're listening. We wouldn't want those little kiddies of yours seeing their daddy getting the shite kicked out of him, would we?"

"All right, Anto, I get the message," he said quickly, hating every second he had to deal with the scumbag. "Leave my kids out of this, though. I'll see you tonight at nine. And this'd better be a sure thing and clear my slate with you, because as soon as I'm in the black, you can fuck right off and crawl back into the hovel you came from."

The sound of thick phlegm being hacked up again had Gary fighting the urge to puke, but he had to wait for Anto to hang up first. Despite his bravado on the phone, he didn't stand a chance when it came to Anto and is cronies. He'd no doubt they'd kick the shit out of him – probably even kill him, given the right circumstances – so he didn't want to piss the bastard off more than he already had.

"Four lame dogs, two absolute bullets," Anto said. "Spread the bets, don't tip the bookies, and don't shorten the odds. Keep the bets at straight forecasts, reap the rewards, and that, my son, is you in the clear. Well, with me, anyhow." He choked out a laugh. "See you after, pal, and don't be late."

The phone line went dead. Gary thought for a minute. *How the hell am I going to pull this one off?* He had to turn up and meet Anto or he was a dead man. But if he told Cathy he had to cancel, he was looking at six months minimum in a full body cast.

"There's only one thing to do," he said to himself, closing his eyes and shaking his head, "I'll have to bring the kids with me."

He shrugged. That mightn't be so bad. He'd often seen children there on a Saturday night, enjoying an evening out with their families. How bad could it be?

"Fuck it, it'll have to do." The back of his neck tingled with a cold sweat as he scrolled through his phone, looking for someone who could spot him a couple of hundred quid to get this bet on and, once and for all, clear his debt.

16th April

Wednesday

Gary swept back the covers on the bed and rubbed the sleep out of his eyes. He checked on the sleeping children before going to the kitchen to make coffee.

It wasn't a bad day outside. He looked out the window and checked the brightening sky, listening to the coffee dripping into the pot below. Without that brew, his day wouldn't officially begin. He stretched his arms above his head, thanking God he was still alive to see the sun rise.

Millie and Jack could have a lie in. After all, it had been after eleven when he'd got them into bed and asleep last night.

As he poured his first cup of fresh coffee, his mind slipped back to last night and the ridiculous risks he'd taken. Shuddering, he remembered bringing the kids through crowds of hardened racegoers, intent on getting his bets on, and his debt cleared. Trying to keep an eye on two six-year-olds had been the hardest part. With crowds of people around, Millie and Jack had done their best to give him a stroke, disappearing behind legs and duffel coats. He'd finally reined them in and stood them up beside the fence, telling them to watch out for dog number eight.

"But there is no number eight, Daddy," Millie squealed, laughing at his silliness.

"Of course there is," he'd said, trying to keep one eye on the betting and the other on two blond heads. He pointed at the track. "You have to watch carefully, quietly. Number eight is the special dog that runs so fast, only the people who concentrate, and don't run off, are able to see him."

"Really?" Jack asked, obviously not buying it.

"When you see him run past," Gary said, realising he'd struck gold on a way of keeping them entertained, "he'll give a little *woof, woof.* But you can only hear it if you're really quiet, and good."

"Keep quiet, Jack," Millie warned, placing her finger to her lips, then giving dirty looks to two men standing nearby who were nearly shouting to each other above the noise of the crowd. "I wish we could get everyone else to shush, too."

Gary knew Millie was about to let a roar at all the other racegoers, so assured her that it was only the people who wanted to see the number-eight dog who had to be good.

"Well, why doesn't everyone want to see him?" she asked, questioned her dad, like any normal six-year-old, until she had a satisfactory answer.

"Because they've all seen him before," Gary explained, a sweat break out on the back of his neck as he watched the odds on his chosen dogs drift.

"But, why wouldn't they want to see him again?" Millie asked.

"Yes, Dad," Jack said, "why wouldn't they all want to win the prize?"

Millie looked at him. "What prize?"

"Well, there must be a prize if you see the golden dog. Right, Dad?"

Keeping his focus on the board, Gary agreed wholeheartedly with Jack. "Uh, huh. Yep, you're spot on there, son."

Millie gave her brother a sideways look full of suspicion. "What's all this about a golden dog?" She turned to Gary. "Did I miss one of the clues?"

Jack frowned at her, as if she was clueless. "It must be golden, Millie, because it's a magic dog that says *woof woof* when it passes, and it knows you're being good – a bit like Santa does. It appears in a puff of smoke, wags its tail, and then flies past. I'm right, Dad, amn't I?" His delight that he'd figured it all out was evident in the pride beaming from his face,

Gary looked at him and had to smile. "Yes, son, that's exactly right. Well done, Jack." His heart melted as he watched the two siblings discuss the golden-dog situation in earnest. He was so lucky to have them in his life. But he needed to get his act together, clear his debts, and take the straight and narrow from now on. These two little people depended on him. They trusted him with their lives, and he needed to take that trust more seriously than he'd been doing.

He looked around, thinking again that it wasn't the best environment for two six-year- olds on a Tuesday night. Then, looking at their heads stuck together in animated conversation, he reckoned it would do them no harm. They treated it like a big adventure. They'd certainly hopped off the coke and hotdogs he'd bought them earlier.

"All right, me auld pal?" The voice from behind brought him back to reality. "Have you got those bets on, or what?"

Gary turned, a tremor running down his legs. "Anto. Yes, ready to go. The money's spread and I'm watching the odds drifting a bit, which is a little worrying. Are you sure about these two hounds? I mean, the rest are definitely lame, right?"

"Lame as ducks," Anto answered, chuckling at his own joke. "Only thing you need to do now is hope to fuck you put the dogs in the right order for the straight forecast. If you did that, then you're quids-in."

A bell rang out as the commentator's voice crackled through the loudspeakers. *"And they're finished loading them now. Thirty seconds and the race is off...and here comes the bunny!"* He finished with a flourish, building the atmosphere to fever pitch.

Gary stood close behind his children, his nerves at hyper-level. The next sixty seconds would be do or die. He crushed the betting slips in his sweaty fist, praying to God Almighty to let him pull this off.

Leaning forward, he whispered in each child's ear, "Keep an eye out for number eight." The mechanical hare whizzed past. "Good Luck."

Millie turned and planted a kiss squarely on his chin. "And good luck to you, too, Daddy," she said before turning back to watch the race.

The commentator's voiced boomed, "And they're off!"

The metal gates shot up on the traps, releasing six yelping greyhounds into the hunt. Twenty-four eager paws kicked up sand as the dogs powered forward. They followed the hare around the steep curve of the first bend. Voices roared all around, all forms of swearing blending into one angry rumble, willing each dog to sprint on and win the race.

Gary was nearly up on his toes as he studied the big screen showing the race. He was counting on dog number two, All Tied Down, and dog number five, Ravenswood Chloe, to finish the race – in that order. The commentator's rapid speech made it difficult to follow who was ahead, but, thankfully, he could just about make out both his dogs being mentioned.

He watched as they took the back stretch, bunched together, and chasing down the bit of fluff that was always out of reach.

Overtaken with excitement, Millie and Jack joined in with the crowd, roaring and squealing. "Come on, number eight," Millie screamed, her face pressed against the wire fence, while Jack gripped the top, bouncing up and down.

At the final bend, all hell broke loose. Two dogs collided on the sharp turn, drawing squeals of pain from number five, Ravenswood Chloe.

"Oh shit!" Gary roared, banging on the fence, forgetting about the little ears in front of him.

All Tied Down sprinted past, racing towards the line, followed half a second behind by number six. Ravenswood Chloe made up the distance, and was clipping the heels of number six for second place.

With less than twenty yards to go, Gary let a few fucks out of him, willing his dog past its rival, needing that result like he'd never needed another.

"Keep going, Jesus, keep going!" he howled, almost afraid to look as the dogs closed in on the finish line.

All Tied Down zipped across the line, easily a length or two ahead, but Gary held his breath as Six and Five battled it out until the bitter end. With neither dog willing to give up second place, they passed under the light – barely a whisker separating them.

"Winner, dog number two, All Tied down," the crackling voice confirmed. "Photo finish for second, dog number five and dog number six."

"Oh, Jesus Christ Almighty," Gary groaned, running both hands through his hair, clutching the handful of betting slips, knowing they could be gold or lead.

"What's wrong, Daddy?" Millie asked, worry in her eyes. "Did you not see the golden dog?"

"We saw it, Dad, didn't we, Millie?" Jack urged, still jumping up and down. Millie, her brows creased in confusion, looked from Jack to Gary.

Jack's eyes filled with excitement as he shook his head. "We saw the golden dog, Dad!" He nudged his sister, nodding for her to play along.

Her mouth fell open when the penny dropped. "Oh, yeah, number eight. It went whizzing past, didn't it, Jack? Winked and everything."

"I definitely heard him barking like mad," Jack confirmed, keeping up the pretence.

"Do we get the prize, Daddy?" they asked together.

Gary just nodded, his eyes glued to the big screen as it showed replay after replay of the finish. He couldn't work out which of the two dogs would be awarded second place. The place judge would decide, and the result would be announced, but until then, he kept his eyes locked on the screen.

"Why is it taking so bloody long?" he asked in frustration. It was too close to call. It looked like his dog had worked hard to catch up, getting his nose in front in the last split second. But it was also clear that dog number six had half a toenail under the finishing light, in the exact same positon.

Feeling light headed, he grabbed the railing for support, ignoring the children's excited chatter as he kept his attention fixed on the screen. It held the answers, and would deal him his fate. He just wished it would hurry up and put him out of this misery.

Then the screen changed and numbers flashed up to confirm the result: first, second, and third.

He tried to focus on the words, but his body buzzed so much the whole screen was a blur. But he could still hear well enough.

The commentator's voice broke through the noise of the crowd. *"Winner, dog number two, All Tied Down."* Gary's head swam. *"Second place…"* His heartbeats thundered through is ears. *"…dog number 5, Ravenswood Chloe, by a nose, and third place, dog number six, Winner Alright, Winner Alright."*

The commentator began reading off odds and bets for the next race. Every other person in the stadium went on about their business. Gary stood, shocked into stillness.

"What's wrong, Daddy?" Jack's voice brought him out of the fog.

He shook his head and focused on his son. "Nothing," he said, letting out the breath he'd been holding, "there's nothing wrong. Everything's grand, lads. No, no, I tell a lie, everything is fantastic!" He flung his arms wide and gathered both children into a celebratory hug. When they finished, he grabbed each by the hand and headed for the row of bookmakers to collect his winnings.

"Let's go and cash in, guys," he said, unable to wipe the smile off his face. "Then we'll go. I think we've had enough excitement for one night."

"Aw, Daddy, we love the dogs," Millie said. "Can we watch another race where they all chase each other?"

"No, love, not tonight." He handed over the betting slips, took his winnings, counted out €1000, and pocketed the rest.

He led them towards the exit, searching the crowd for Anto. "We need to meet someone now, lads, just for minute. Then we're going home."

"Who is it you need to meet, Dad?" Jack asked. "Is it your friend?"

"No, Jack, this fella is not my friend. I just need to do a bit of business with him."

"Do we get our prize, too?" Millie asked.

Gary looked down at her. "What?"

"Because we saw the magic number-eight dog, Daddy. Do we get a prize as well?"

Both looked up at him, eyes wide, and he recognised every bar of himself when he was pulling a fast one. He couldn't help laughing.

"Let's get this other bit of business sorted first, then we'll see what prize you can pick out in the toy shop tomorrow. Okay?"

"Oh, really, Daddy?" Millie squealed, bouncing with excitement.

"Anything you want," he said, "but first, let me talk to this fella, then we can get going. And, erm, lads," he paused and glanced around, "let's just keep all this between ourselves. It's our little secret, right? No need for Mammy to know, right?"

The children nodded, ready to agree with anything their daddy said to them.

***

The whole night had been a rollercoaster from start to finish. Now, with the fanfare over, Gary shook as he realised how close he'd come to losing everything. For those few minutes as the photo-finish was decided, his whole future lay in the hands of a faceless judge. Even after all his mistakes in the past, waiting for that result had brought clarity to his dire situation. He needed to get his act together. Two children were depending on him. Having them with him last night was the kick up the arse he needed to cop himself on.

He refilled his coffee mug and did some calculations in his head, figuring what he owed, and to whom. This needed to stop. He couldn't continue living on a knife edge, no matter what type of buzz winning gave him.

The cheque he'd got from Sam last year had cleared the previous debts, but gambling was in his DNA – he couldn't help it. He got such a thrill from the chase and couldn't stop himself racking up new debts as he fed his habit.

But now he needed to toe the line. He was positive the little business deal he'd set in motion last week would turn a profit soon. That would start him off nicely.

"I'm getting myself sorted, this time," he said to the empty kitchen. "No more ducking and diving."

"Are we getting a duck?" a sleepy voice asked, startling him.

"What?" He turned to see Millie in her fleecy sleepsuit, her blond hair a mass of tangles. "No, sweetheart, we're not getting a duck."

"But you just said about the ducking?" Her gaze flicked to the ceiling. "Or is that a swear word?" She slapped a hand over her mouth, her eyes wide.

Gary hugged her, kissing the top of her head. "Don't worry about it, love. Ducking is not a swear word. Now, where's your brother? I'm doing pancakes for breakfast. Would you like that?"

"Oh yeah, deadly." She called for Jack as she ran to wake him.

Gary set about making breakfast. He was well into it when the children entered the kitchen, with Jack urging Millie forward. It was obvious they were on a mission.

Millie glanced back at her brother before moving over to the counter. "Daddy, after pancakes, are we going to get our prize?"

Gary knew better than to think they'd forgotten. "Sure." He poured another round of batter onto the hot pan. "Let's go into town and you can pick out your prizes."

"So far," Jack said, rubbing the sleep out of his eyes, "this is the best day ever."

Gary sorted the breakfast, happy that for once things had worked in his favour. Listening to Millie and Jack organise the rest of the day made him realise how simple their needs really were. All they wanted was love and affection, with the odd prize for spotting the golden dog at the racetrack thrown in.

17th April

Thursday

Cathy hadn't felt this lonely in years. With Sam still away, and the children at Gary's, the quietness of the house over the past two days had begun to weigh on her. Checking the clock for what must have been the umpteenth time, she decided to text Byron to see if she was free for lunch.

> *Hey, girl. Want to meet for quick lunch, if u have time? C x*

She waited a few minutes for a reply, pacing around the kitchen and checking the fridge and cupboards. Her phone pinged.

> *Sure, only have 1 hr, is 2o'clock ok?*

> *Perfect, will meet u in café around corner from ur office? X x*

Several long minutes passed before her phone pinged again.

> *Ok, c u then.*

Cathy squinted at the phone. Something wasn't right. She went through the messages again. Was she misreading them? Normally, any correspondence between them was littered with emoji's and exclamation points, with every text ending with an x.

"Something's up," she said to herself as she began wiping down the kitchen counters, until she realised she'd already done them all. She took a deep breath and put the kettle on for a cup of tea.

At six weeks and five days pregnant, she'd hoped the dreadful morning sickness would have eased off, but it was still causing problems. However, this morning, she'd finally tolerated some dry toast, and now she felt confident enough to give black tea a go.

She dug her phone from her bag and texted Sam, not for the first time that day.

> *Hey you. Me again. Bored without you. Meeting Byron for lunch. What you doing?*

She made her tea while she waited, which wasn't for long. Her phone pinged.

> *U should be resting while you can. No point wasting a child free house. Get some sleep. Rest your body. How is the stomach now?*

She loved how concerned he was about her, but didn't know if she could stand it long-term. She texted back: *Ok, keeping down toast. Having tea now, no problems. Have u calmed down with Sorcha yet? Did you see her yesterday?*

Her tea was good, and her stomach didn't have issues with it, either. Her phone pinged: *Ffs don't talk to me. Little wagon knew what she was doing. I walked right into that one, didn't I? Had a think about it. I will have to bite the bullet and bring her.*

She shook her head, disgusted that Sam was being taken advantage of, and by a conniving little wagon like Sorcha.

Really, do you think you should let her away with treating u like that?

While she waited for his reply, she took a couple of biscuits out and tried one with her tea. *Hmm...things are looking up.*

His message came through: *I know, but you know the situation. It's like I am abandoning her again by moving back to Ireland. This weekend away with her won't kill me. It's one last treat from me. What you think?*

She wanted to tell him exactly what she thought. Sorcha was a conniving, selfish, gold-digging wagon. Sam was letting her walk all over him and it irked her bigtime, even though she knew he could see what was going on. She understood why he was willing to tolerate it, but it still bugged her.

She considered her words before replying: *It's a funny one for sure. You were definitely tricked into agreeing to it, and you're right, what harm can it do? It's just this one time, right?*

She hoped that was the case. The thought that Sam might find himself trapped in an emotionally fraught bind with his daughter, especially now that he was going to be a father again, was too much to take.

His reply came through: *Yes, just the one weekend, in June I think. I'm all yours before then and forever after.*

The way she read that, it sounded like Sam felt he was giving up Sorcha for her benefit. That didn't sit well with her and was something they would have to discuss when he got home. She didn't want to get into it by text so, for the moment, she let the subject drop. Then something dawned on her. Byron's wedding was in June. *Crap!* She texted him back: *What date in June is the concert? Byron and Toms wedding is June. Better not be the same weekend???*

His response didn't take long: *I don't know but will find out. What date the wedding?*

She had to think about that, just to be sure: *Saturday 21st, 3rd weekend in June. Do not dare leave me alone and pregnant at my best friend's wedding. I will kill you.*

It took some time for Sam's reply to hit her inbox: *Leave it with me Cathy. Don't get mad. Have to go, need to keep packing or will never get home. Ring u later x x x*

"Just brilliant," she said. She sipped her tea, now worrying how all her plans could be ruined because of that spoilt little bitch.

With her diary opened out on the table, she counted forward the weeks to Byron's big day. On June 21st, she'd be exactly sixteen weeks pregnant. There was no getting away from the fact that her bump would be noticed at that stage, but there wasn't a chance she was being left to answer a battery of questions about the baby alone, and to field explanations about the father's absence, too. *No, Sam is going, and that's that.*

"Four months pregnant." She sighed as she googled it on her phone. What would she look like? The images popped up in the gallery. Sixteen weeks. "Wow, look at that." She read the description printed underneath: *Baby will be the size of a small apple.*

She rubbed her flat belly, then lifted her shirt to look at her bellybutton. "That means you're now only the size of a pip. Three or four inches long at sixteen weeks, eh? Do you think I'll still be able to fit into that slinky black bridesmaid dress Byron picked out for us?"

As hard as she tried, it was difficult to remember how things were during the early days of her pregnancy on Millie and Jack. Her time towards the end, though, was etched in her memory – she'd nearly burst out of her skin. Perhaps when you live in leggings and t-shirts for the duration, you don't really notice your size until one day you no longer fit behind the steering wheel of your car.

But for this pregnancy, she supposed, with a single baby, it would be different. She'd be smaller – that was for sure. According to the website, her body would be showing at the very least a little bump, but still big enough not to be easily disguised in a form-fitting satin number. She didn't want to worry about all that now. No, she'd cross that bridge when she came to it. For now, she needed to nail down Sam with a date for this concert with Sorcha, and pray to God it didn't clash with the wedding.

By two o'clock, she was sitting at a window table in the café, starving. She ordered a plain scone with Jam, with a pot of green tea, hoping her stomach would continue to behave. The last thing she wanted was her lunch with Byron to be ruined by having to run to the bathroom every five minutes.

The waitress returned with her food, followed close behind by Byron, who ordered a BLT and latte as she sat across from Cathy.

Cath took one look at her friend and knew right away that something was wrong. Dark shadows smudged Byron's normally bright eyes, causing her to look tired and drawn – nowhere near what you'd expect from a glowing bride-to-be. If anything, this wedding was putting too much stress on Byron and Tom, and Cathy wondered how they could possibly be enjoying any of it.

"I'm fine," Byron said, dismissing Cathy's concern with a wave of her hand. "I've just got a lot on my mind." She glanced around. "Wedding stuff."

Cathy felt a definite chill as Byron shot her a curt look while she poured a glass of water for herself. *What's going on here?*

"Is there anything I can help you with?" she asked.

Byron took a sip of her water, then wiped her mouth with a napkin. "No, I don't think so." She looked out the window. "There's a lot of running around involved. Invitations, menu planning, leaflets for the church – that sort of thing."

Cathy hated seeing Byron in such bad form, and knew there must be something she could do to take the pressure off.

"Let me do the invitations, then. Give me the address of the printers and I'll go collect them for you. Then you can come down to my house some evening and I'll help you write and stuff envelopes."

Byron remained silent as her food was delivered. Then, instead of responding to Cathy's helpful offer, she closed her eyes and bit into her BLT.

"I can do the church leaflet, if you like?" Cathy said, ploughing on with the next suggestion, more than willing to try a different tack. "Something nice and fancy, with romantic poems and sentimental memories. Something for all the family." She grinned at her own joke. "I'll even emboss two doves onto each cover, with intertwining gold rings in their beaks. What do you think?"

Byron shook her head. "I'd prefer to do that myself, if you don't mind? It's more personal."

Cathy stalled, sure there was something else going on here, but until she knew what it was, all she could do was try again.

"Okay, can I give you a hand with booking the cars, choosing the flowers, briefing the band? Anything?" She leaned forward, frustration burning into her chest at the look of indifference on Byron's face. *What's going on?* She was pussyfooting around Byron, trying not to piss her off, when she had more than enough on her own plate.

"Cathy, I don't need your help, thank you. It's all under control. This is myself and Tom's wedding and I want to enjoy it. Can you please just let me have that pleasure without trying to take over with the preparations as well?"

Cathy's mouth dropped open. Never before had she heard Byron speak to anyone like that, especially her. Annabel, she would expect it from, but not Byron. Heat worked its way up her neck and into her face. She sat back. "What's going on here, Byron? I don't understand. I'm offering to help you with a few bits and pieces, not walk down the aisle with Tom."

Fire flared in her friend's eyes. It was just a flicker, but it was there.

"Pffff, as if that would ever happen." Byron's words dripped with sarcasm.

Cathy couldn't believe what she was hearing. It took a moment to realise that her friend was actually angry at her, not the wedding preparations or the stress, but directly at her. And for the life of her, she couldn't understand why.

She took a deep breath and waited until Byron looked her in the eye. What she saw was hurt, and this made her worry. What the hell had she done to cause her best friend to react like this?

"Listen to me, By." She kept her tone gentle, wanting to get to the bottom of whatever this craziness was. "There is obviously something going on here. It's clear you're totally pissed off at me, and for once I haven't one clue as to what I'm supposed to have done to annoy you so much that you spoke to me like that. Like I'm dirt." A thought struck her. "Are you angry that I'm your maid of honour and I mightn't be able to fit into the expensive designer dress you bought for me? Because, if that's it, I'm sure I can wear hold-me-in knickers, or something. There must be a seam allowance we can work with – all dresses have them now. We can have a look," she said, trying to turn the disaster with the dress around, "and if all fails, I'll pay for a new dress and the slinky black number can go with you on your honeymoon cruise. It would look fabulous when you're invited to the captain's table."

She eyed Byron. The woman's stiff posture and thin lips told her the dress-fitting wasn't the problem here.

Byron kept quiet, her jaw set on edge, her cheeks flushed.

Cathy threw her hands up. She wanted to grab hold of her and shake the truth right out. "Why are you not talking to me, Byron? What is it? What have I done?" She blinked back tears of confusion. "I'm not

161

a mind reader. If I don't know what I'm supposed to have done, how can I possibly make it right?"

"You've done enough, Cathy," Byron said, not looking her in the eye. "I don't need your help with the wedding." She flung her words across the table, hitting Cathy straight in the heart. "I don't care about the mass booklets or the bloody invitations, and I couldn't give a damn if the shagging dress looks like a sack of potatoes on you. I just don't care. Now, can we leave it at that?"

Anger surged through Cathy and she leaned forward, shocked at being spoken to like a child, and by her best friend of all people. "No, we most certainly cannot leave it at that."

Bryon shook her head, indicating she'd had enough. She pulled a note from her purse and left it on the table beside her half-eaten BLT. Then she gathered her coat and bag and stood up.

"I can't deal with this right now." She kept her voice low, perhaps embarrassed by her earlier outburst. "I think I'd better leave."

She moved towards the door and Cathy got up and caught her by the arm. "Byron, for God's sake, talk to me. Please! This is me and you, Byron. You need to tell me what's going on here. Why are you so upset with me?" Tears welled again.

Byron looked at her for a moment, and Cathy thought she was ready to speak. Then she turned away and strode out of the café, leaving her standing there, dumbfounded.

She sat back on her seat, utterly shocked. Byron walked past the window, her head down. Cathy could tell she was crying. She unlocked her phone and speed-dialled her number, and wasn't surprised when the call went straight to voicemail.

What the hell? She shouldered her bag, left a ten-euro note on the table for her food, then moved outside into the street, where she waited for the beep at the end of Byron's voicemail recording.

Taking a deep breath, she let the words flow, "Byron, what's going on? Please tell me. I know things got a bit heated back there, but I honestly don't know what I've done. It couldn't be that bad, for God's sake." She spoke quickly, trying to get the full message in before the phone cut her off. "Ring me back," she begged, "and we'll talk. I hate this. You're my best friend and you're getting married. I want to be there for you, but I need to know how to fix this. Look, please call me and we'll talk, okay? I love you. Ring me back... Bye."

Confused and upset, she walked back to her car with tears rolling down her face. This was certainly not the ending she'd imagined when she'd decided to meet her friend for lunch. But it was up to Byron now. She could do no more until the woman she thought was her best friend started to play ball and give her a shot at clearing up whatever this mess was about.

18th April

Friday

Annabel planned to finish work early. She wanted to go shopping. Jean Luc was coming home tomorrow and she decided to treat herself to some beauty treatments, and maybe some new sexy lingerie.

When she collected him from the airport, the first port of call would be her apartment. Her pulse raced as she remembered how skilful he was in their lovemaking, caressing her body like a fragile piece of china, turning her on, then stoking her fire.

Jean Luc knew exactly what she liked, masterfully satisfying her not only between the sheets, but in the shower, on the couch, or wherever – once he gave her his smouldering look, that was it – she was finished.

A sharp knock on her office door pulled her out of the erotic daydream.

"Come in," she said, moving some files around her desk.

Ms Connolly. The woman, in her mid-forties, took the seat offered by Annabel.

"Annabel, how are you?"

Why was her senior manager paying her a visit on a Friday afternoon? She swallowed back the nervous lump in her throat without making it too evident. "Very well, Ms Connolly, and you?"

This woman was the living embodiment of all work and no play. She lived for her work and, despite the perfectly coiffed hair and designer business suits, Sandra Connolly was well able to hold her own in a boardroom full of testosterone. Everyone knew she was a career woman, with no time for relationships or family. Very few people liked this woman, and even fewer would admit to being her friend. She had successfully removed several members of staff, with little or no loyalty to their years of service, just because they failed to maintain the rigorous targets imposed on them. To her, there was no room for failure, no second chances. Her belief in absolute perfection was renowned throughout the company. Nobody dared to cross or disagree with this woman. It was more than their job was worth.

"What can I do for you, Ms Connolly?" Annabel asked.

"Please call me Sandra, Annabel," she said. "I just wanted to thank you in person for the Trojan work you did on those fraud cases."

Annabel couldn't believe her ears. "It was my pleasure. Was everything okay? I mean, I think I gave a fairly accurate, detailed report on each file. Information which you can use, going forward. I don't think there should be any further issues with these clients, once they are compensated."

"Yes, indeed," Sandra said, "in your work, you have prevented several lawsuits from forming against this company, and possible media damage if the details were ever made public."

Annabel leaned forward, wanting to stress her point, "My discretion is guaranteed, Sandra."

Sandra Connolly nodded, her sharp eyes reading every strained muscle and twitch Annabel made.

"Just one thing, Annabel," she said, her eyes narrowing. "How did those files come to be in your possession? Not one of these cases was a previous client of yours."

Annabel shifted back, unsure of where this conversation was going. She decided to be upfront and honest. No point trying to cover anything up where Ms Connolly was concerned. The woman had x-ray vision and saw through everything.

"I was told by a colleague that you specifically requested that I work on them." She clenched her toes to stop her legs trembling. "Was that not correct, because if I've done something out of place, please—"

"No, no, your work is good, Annabel, and I thank you." She rose from the chair in a graceful movement, placing one high-heeled foot in front of the other as she turned to leave. "One last thing that I am obliged to let you know." She looked back. "I find it disturbing that you had time to complete so many complex reports on such short notice. In doing so, you have either ignored your existing clients, or maybe it's because there is truth in what I'm hearing."

Annabel stood up, shocked to her core. "I don't understand, Sandra. What have you heard?"

"Late-night meetings with elderly gentlemen, coupled with mismanaged funds, all covered up so expertly it has never been picked up by auditors. Seems to me like it's an inside job, executed by someone so skilful she has managed to get away with it until now."

Annabel tried to move forward on shaking legs. She had to explain about the bitch Gemma and the rumours she'd started but, in her shock, words wouldn't come.

Having delivered her warning, and seeing that nothing was forthcoming from Annabel in her defence, Sandra turned and walked out of the office.

Annabel almost collapsed into the vacated chair, her head spinning as a wave of nausea washed over her. *What the hell has just happened?* "Jesus Christ, this is deadly serious." She grasped at the desk, looking for her phone. Her hand shook as she scrolled down and made a call. It went straight to voicemail. "Gemma, you little bitch. I'll make you pay." She grabbed up her coat and bag, then ran for the door.

19th April

Saturday

Annabel turned over and stretched in her bed. Still half asleep, she wondered why her leg hit something hard. She sat up, ready to bolt, then remembered that Jean Luc was lying beside her.

She sighed with satisfied calmness as she checked the bedside clock. 7.45 p.m. blinked back at her as she sneaked out of bed and headed for the bathroom.

The flimsy black negligee fell to the floor before she stepped into the steaming shower. She worked citrus shampoo through her hair, massaging her scalp and moaning as images of Jean Luc lying in her bed flooded her mind. Memories of the afternoon they'd spent pleasuring each other set off a tingling sensation between her legs that had her quivering inside.

A sweet-smelling shower cream replaced his scent on her body as she stroked every inch of her skin with a natural-fibre loofa, cleansing and buffing herself until she glowed.

She stepped out of the shower, more turned on than she'd been in months. Jean Luc had brought her to a climax several times already, but now, the need to satisfy threatened to consume her.

Still wet, she walked straight to Jean Luc, lying fast asleep in the middle of the bed. Shy and unsure, she hesitated, wondering if she should let him sleep, but then his eyes opened and he looked directly at her, as if delving into her mind.

Raw heat radiated from his body, and the slight quirk of his mouth told Annabel he was ready for more.

She pulled back the duvet, revealing his naked body, and climbed onto the bed, taking his hard length in one hand. A soft moan escaped his lips, but otherwise, he remained silent, his head resting on pillows, his eyes closed. Annabel kissed the throbbing pulse on his neck, then licked his hot smooth skin. Still stroking him, she straddled his hips and leaned forward to let her heavy breasts graze his chest.

Her tight, puckered nipples rubbed against chest hair, sending exquisite shivers through her body. She nipped playfully at his jaw, then his arms came around her, pulling her close.

She savoured his mouth in a plundering dance of tongues and lips, eyes closed, drinking him in, deeply connected through the heat of shared breath.

In this position, she felt strong and in control, but she wanted to both make and take the pleasure, so she took Jean Luc's hands from her back and brought them up over his head, holding them there with one of hers.

He laughed. "Oh, feeling a bit of Fifty Shades, are you? Do you want to tie me up? Punish me?"

"Not a bad idea," she whispered in his ear, stretching down again to take him in a firm grip. She laid her body over his, soft and supple as she continued to kiss and caress him.

Even though he wasn't actually doing anything, his desire oozed from every pore, making her ache from deep within. Just knowing he needed her gave her so much pleasure. She was soaking as she straddled him again, only this time she slid him in, slow and easy, until he was in to the hilt.

Jean Luc's breath quickened as she worked him, gripping him from inside as she gyrated, squeezing his hips with her strong legs as she rode him towards climax. Small pants of pleasure passed through his lips as he bucked in time to her movements.

Annabel sensed his resolve fracturing and increased her pace, keeping the rhythm strong until she was sure he was about to come. She wanted him to shoot into her so she could milk every drop from him.

At what seemed the last moment, just when she was sure Jean Luc was about to explode, he ripped his hands free, grabbed her hips, and flipped her over. Now he was straddling her.

"Jean Luc, no!"

"Ah, but yes, Mon Cheri," he said, catching his breath, sweat dripping from his forehead. "You tried to take me by surprise, unprepared, but that is not the way it is going to be."

"I'm sorry, my darling," she whispered, wriggling under his weight, her mound connecting with the heat of his balls. "Have I been a naughty girl? Do you need to punish me?"

Jean Luc let out a long, vocal breath, his cock twitching, rock-hard over her. "Jesus, Annabel, you're killing me. You trapped me in a delicate position, Bella. Now I must have my revenge."

His sexy smile and raised eyebrow told her she had no hope of escape. Not that she wanted to. She needed this man to dull the ache threatening to overtake her. It wouldn't take much to make her scream, but now Jean Luc was torturing her, making her wait.

He caressed her body with slow, gentle strokes, kissing each puckered nipple, nibbling and sucking until her breasts ached. With a growl of frustration, she reached down to hold him, to guide him, but like she'd done before, he pushed both her hands above her head. With her body now taut, she arched her back and spread her legs, wanting him to pleasure her from deep within.

Jean Luc didn't disappoint, licking and plunging, biting and riding, right through to her core, hitting every raw nerve and fibre with his powerful strokes.

She thought she couldn't take much more as she threw her head back in sheer ecstatic delight, her body covered in glistening sweat. With eyes closed and hands grasping the top of the bed, she wrapped her legs around her man and screamed into the universe as he pounded her, roaring that he was about to come, and she felt the heat of his seed as she collapsed into herself with the sweetest release, again and again, until she was a quivering mess beneath her French delight.

She didn't know how long it took before she opened her eyes, but each step down from cloud nine had taken a most-pleasurable lifetime. Jean Luc raised his head, a grin of satisfaction spread across his handsome face. Annabel breathed out a whispery, "thank you," before falling back against the pillows and into a well-deserved slumber.

A long satisfying sleep later, she was woken by a kiss on her temple. "Bonjour, mo petite. Are you still alive? You have slept all day."

Her heart flipped as she saw the genuine concern on his face, coupled with the cup of hot tea in his hand.

"Wow," was all she could manage.

"Yes, indeed, wow," he said as she sat up and took the mug of steaming brew from him. "That was very special, Annie. It was the best welcome home I could have hoped for."

Blushing to her roots, she remembered her forwardness and total inhibition involved in their last lovemaking session. She shyly turned her face away.

One gentle finger under her chin brought her back to face him. "What we have here," he whispered, "is very, very special, and I want to say this to you now."

Holding a breath, she focused on his eyes, full of sincerity and hope.

"Annabel Clancy, Je taime de tout mon Coeur, corps et ame. Sans toi je suis vide et seul. Vous remplissez mon Coeur avec tant de passion, de sorte, mich jeie, je sens que je deus voler."

Annabel stared into his eyes, unable to understand one single word. But the words didn't matter. She felt every sentiment, every loving intention, like he was speaking the language of love, and she was fluent at that.

She cupped his face, wanting him to know that she felt the same. "I love you, too, Jean Luc. I love you with all my heart. You make me feel safe and secure. I can trust, I can run free, I can act a little silly if I want to. We're not two separate people, Jean Luc, we're supposed to be two halves of the same heart. Deep down in my very essence, I know you're the one person I cannot be without. My life is complete while you are with me."

Simply by kissing her on the mouth, she knew he agreed. She relaxed back, letting the love wash over them, wanting to remember this exact moment for the rest of her life.

The doorbell rang. "Bugger! Who's that at this hour?" she asked, wrapping the duvet around herself.

"I ordered Chinese food," Jean Luc said, heading for the door. "It is your favourite, yes? Go take a shower and meet me on the sofa."

Ten minutes later, wrapped in a thick towelling bathrobe, Annabel plucked food out of takeaway boxes and dropped it on her plate. "It tastes so good," she said around a mouthful of Singapore noodles, letting the spicy flavour roll over her tongue.

"You are hungry, my Annabel, after all your exercise." He smiled as he poured her a glass of crisp white wine.

***

Jean Luc was happy to see her relaxed and enjoying herself. He sensed there was something causing her distress, but now was not the time to delve into all that. At least for tonight, he wanted to keep her calm and trouble free. Tomorrow he would question her further, raising his concerns about how stressed she sounded each night on the phone, and how he almost didn't recognise her earlier at the airport. A gaunt and trembling woman had met him at arrivals, wrapped in a state of constant anxiety, it was a wonder she could function at all. But all that for tomorrow. He watched her demolishing a carton of sweet and sour pork. Tonight he vowed to show her how committed he was, hoping to perhaps in some small way take that worry off her shoulders.

Yes, tomorrow would be time enough to delve into whatever had happened to her over the past six weeks.

20th April

Sunday

"He came, Mammy, he came." Two excited children raced across the floor towards her, each holding an Easter egg in boxes nearly bigger than themselves.

Cathy shook her head. *I'll bloody-well kill Becky, picking out Easter eggs like that.* She opened both arms out, showing the children a look of surprise and amusement.

"Oh, my goodness," she said, sharing in the excitement, "how lucky are you guys? The Easter Bunny must really like you."

"I know," Millie cried, twirling a fancy circle, holding the chocolate prize high above her head.

"I'm going to eat mine now," Jack declared. Elaborate cardboard wrapping was wasted on him as he tore the packaging to shreds, digging deep to get to the chocolate treasure inside.

Normally, Cathy would insist on a healthy breakfast before the children were allowed any sort of treats. However, she always made an exception on Easter Sunday and Christmas morning.

"Jesus," she once said when her own mother pulled her up on it, "they're only children for a few short years. They need to break the rules and enjoy themselves every now and then. And anyway, the chocolate tastes so much better when you know you shouldn't be eating it."

So, keeping with tradition, Jack bit into the giant egg, sending a spray of broken chocolate in an arch around him.

"Don't worry, Mammy," he said, inspecting the damage, "I'll pick up every last bit."

Cathy laughed at her son, the little guy sitting cross-legged on the kitchen floor, savouring every single morsel of the rich treat.

She noticed that Millie had taken a more refined approach to enjoying her egg, extracting the foil-wrapped chocolate from its casing like it was a crystal ornament, whispering to herself as she set it on the table.

Totally focused, her head cocked to one side, she used two hands to add up an impossible amount of numbers, finally giving up and asking Cathy for help. "How many days till Christmas?"

"Eh, I'm not sure, pet. It's a good while away yet."

"Oh, well, can you google it, please?" Her blue eyes were now pleading weapons.

"All right, Millie, but why do you want to know?" She reached for her phone to check on the calculator app.

"Well," Millie said, matter-of-factly, "if I break this egg into little pieces, then I can have chocolate for breakfast every day until Christmas." She stretched up to see the screen on the phone. "How many days does it say?"

A smile spread across Cathy's face. *Where does this child come up with her ideas? Top marks for inventiveness.* Trying to keep a straight face was hard as she read out the required information.

"It says here, 249 days until Christmas, Millie. Do you think you can count to that number on your own?"

She knew there wasn't a hope in hell that Easter egg would last more than one day, never mind 249. A small frown crossed Millie's brow as she concentrated on the puzzle before her.

"All right," she finally said, "better get to work, so." She smashed the egg onto the wooden kitchen table, shattering the chocolate into several large pieces. "Okay, that's how many? One, two, three, four, five, six, seven…eight." She shook her head. "Not enough." She broke the bigger pieces into smaller and smaller shards, giggling to herself. "Gonna need a few more bits than this."

Cathy watched as she worked her way through a chocolate maths' equation, wondering when the child would finally give in and just eat the damn thing.

Jack looked up, perhaps wondering if he should follow suit, but then just shrugged and continued to eat.

Wrapping herself in a personal hug, Cathy watched them do their chocolaty thing. While she cherished every second she got to spend with her children, it was moments like this that she loved the most. Easter Sunday morning, everyone still in their pyjamas, chocolate all over little hands and faces, with pure delight flowing from childish giggles. These were the moments that mattered, and that would hopefully last a lifetime.

Sam arrived at the house in the afternoon, bringing with him two more eggs, spotted by the children before he even got out of the car.

"Sam, Sam," they squealed, dancing around him, hooked up on sugar and getting more excited by the second.

"Are they for us?" Jack asked.

"Yes," Sam answered, handing over the chocolate treats. "Happy Easter, you guys."

Millie and Jack flung their arms around his waist, knocking him backwards against the wall.

"Thanks, Uncle Sam," Millie said, before they turned and raced back into the house.

"Don't eat them all at once," he called after them, but his words fell on deaf ears.

"Too late," Cathy said, smiling brightly as she strode towards him, delighted he was here to share the day. "They've already demolished giant eggs the Easter Bunny, or should I say, Becky, brought them. We've had chocolate for breakfast and lunch so far. I'm hoping I can get some real food into them for dinner."

Sam faltered. "I…ah, hope you don't mind the Easter eggs."

Cathy slid her arms around his waist. "Not at all. I can manage the children on a sugar rush for one day. It's only twice a year, if you include Christmas. Anyway, Gary has them tomorrow, so let them have a bit of fun now, and he can deal with them coming down off their high on his time."

"Oh, you are an evil one," Sam said, pulling her close and nuzzling her neck. "Hooking the children up and then passing them onto their dad to deal with."

She pulled back to look at his face. "Let him be the responsible parent for once. I'm always having to deal with tantrums and strops, and then Gary just swoops in and gives them everything they ask for. Let him see what the hard part of parenting is like for once."

Sam touched her face with the back of his fingers. "You really are the vengeful ex-wife, aren't you? A woman scorned, and all that." He chuckled and kissed her cheek. "Must remember not to tick you off in future."

She grinned and kissed him back. "Don't you forget it, mister, or I'll have to punish you, too." A shiver travelled down her spine when her hip rubbed against the hardness in his trousers.

"Later, babe," he said, leaning into the car and coming out with a bouquet of flowers. "I'll show you exactly what you can do to punish me."

"Oh, I love flowers." She took them and savoured the cocktail of scents that brought her straight back to the fields of her childhood. "Gorgeous, but don't think this is going to get you off the hook." She led him into the house to help manage two hyper-active, very happy children.

21st April

Monday

Gary parked the car and walked up to Cathy, who was waiting at her front door.

"They're nearly ready," she said. "Do you want to come in for a minute?"

He hesitated. She'd mentioned earlier that Sam was back in Ireland. "Is he in there?" He flicked a look past her into the house.

"No," she answered, "Sam's gone to visit his parents."

He stepped forward as two bouncing bundles of energy raced towards him and leaped into his arms.

"Daddy, Daddy, you're here," they cried, their eyes wide in sheer excitement.

"Hey, little munchkins, did the Easter bunny come?" He couldn't miss the chocolate smears around their mouths.

"Yes," Millie answered. "One huge egg, with lots of little ones, and Granny and Grandad gave us one as well."

"And Sam," Jack added.

A nerve twitched in Gary's face at the sound of Sam's name coming from his son's mouth.

"Well," he said, recovering quickly, "do you know what happened in my house? I got up yesterday

181

morning and found two massive Easter eggs at the end of my bed."

Millie's eyes widened. "No way," she said, clapping with delight.

Jack shoved her aside. "Well, that was very, very kind of the bunny," he said. "He must know how good we are when we're at Dad's house. Right, Dad?"

Light dawned on Millie's face. She elbowed her way ahead of Jack. "Are they really for us, Daddy?"

Gary winked at Cathy, relishing this rare family moment. "I'm pretty sure they're not for me." He remained on his hunkers as he explained the situation. "One is a chocolate-buttons' egg, with an Elsa doll attached, and the other one is filled with M&Ms, with what looks like a new football sitting beside it."

Jack swayed, and Cathy reached out to steady him, then eased him towards a chair. She knelt and rubbed his back. "Sorry, they've had a lot of chocolate again today. I think it's time for some real food. I'll go make sandwiches." She checked Jack's face, smiling when a bit of colour returned, then got up and went to the kitchen.

Gary kept an eye on Jack for a few more minutes, chatting with the two of them about what they'd do later on in his house.

Cathy asked if he'd like something to eat. He followed the voice into the kitchen, where she was arranging sliced cheese onto buttered bread.

"Eh, yeah, why not?" His stomach rumbled as his eyes devouring the tasty-looking sandwiches. He hadn't eaten yet, and it had been a long time since there'd been bread as fresh as this in his place.

Staying quiet, he watched as Cathy continued to prepare the sandwiches, garnishing each side plate with crisps, then pouring glasses of milk for each of them.

Spending the bit of time here, with his children and Cathy, reminded him so much of happier times. They'd had great fun together. Days like this, where the most boring thing in the world, like a cheese sandwich, could evoke a thousand memories. But then he'd gone and wrecked it all. His affairs and gambling had destroyed his marriage and ruined his life.

Sure, he got to see the children and have them visit, but he missed *this*. He missed them being together, as a family – warm and secure – Millie and Jack, being here with both their parents, having fun, sharing stories, making memories. Together.

Regret ripped at his gut as he thought of all he'd lost. *I've fucked it up, bigtime. Threw away the best thing I ever had.* All those women he'd slept with. Where were they now? Tramps, most of them, who couldn't hold a candle to the woman standing in front of him.

Being young and good-looking was no excuse for the way he'd acted. What a dickhead. But he wanted it all back now, everything he'd lost, his home, his children, his wife. He wanted his wife. Cathy. Strong and confident, and well able to handle whatever life threw at her.

He wanted his memories back: the good, the bad, even the ugly. He wanted his family.

"Gary? Gary, are you even listening to me?"

"Huh? Oh, yeah, cheese is grand."

She frowned. "I asked if you wanted coffee or water."

"Coffee, please. Here, I'll make it, you have your hands full there." He moving to fill the kettle and get mugs out of the press.

"Thanks," she said, then pointed behind her. "No, the mugs are in this press now."

He looked at her, sure she could read the hurt on his face as he acknowledged with a nod that things had changed since he'd lived here. Cathy had moved on.

"Look," she said, "I know this is hard on you, seeing the children with another man. Being in your old home, knowing Sam could walk in the door at any moment…"

He glanced at the front door, expecting Sam to walk in, right on cue.

"...but you are Millie and Jack's dad." She spoke gently, as if explaining something difficult to a child. "No matter who's here, Gary, it will always be you they go to when they're older. Looking for money, or learning to drive, or maybe just to give out about me." She rolled her eyes at that. "You are, and always will be, their dad. I won't ever let them forget that."

Unsure if his voice would hold if he spoke, he took a deep breath, nodding in agreement with all she'd said.

She continued, "Really, you don't need to be buying them all sorts of expensive toys. They have plenty of stuff. Millie already has every single item that was ever released from that Frozen phenomena, and a ball is a ball as far as Jack's concerned. He doesn't care if it comes from Tesco or Manchester United. Once it's round and has air in it, he's happy."

"Yeah, I know." He coughed out the knot in his throat.

"And those other toys you bought during the week?"

He moved out of her eye-line before she saw the guilty flush rising up his neck. "Eh, well, that was nothing. I just happened to be passing the shop and popped in for a minute. Spur of the moment, like."

"Either way," she said, "Millie and Jack don't need all that stuff. They want your time, your love, your affection, preferably on a regular basis, not this chopping and changing from one week to the next. It's confusing them."

"I know, I know." *Why is she going on like this?* Maybe it was time to explain his plan for the future. "It's been a bit messed up since I finished working at the pub. I'm taking it one day at a time. A bit of work here, another bit there, but I'm hoping to have a steady position lined up in the next few weeks. There's the real possibility of something with a bit of stability, workwise, coming down the line. I'm just waiting to hear from a fella about it."

He knew she was letting him off lightly. If the roles were reversed, he'd be flipping his lid right now. But the truth was, he now wanted to get his life back on track, turn the corner, jump back on the straight and narrow and let it take him to better places. He wanted Cathy to realise how good they could be, together again, as a family.

Stepping closer, he reached out to take her hand.

She moved back. "What are you doing?"

"Cathy, I've told you before, but I'll say it again…" He took a deep breath and inched closer. "I still love you. Can we make a family here again?"

She began to protest but he cut her off.

"Look, I know I made a balls of it before. I hurt you. But things have changed. I've changed."

She stared back at him, her mouth open.

"I'm trying, Cathy, really, I am." He caught hold of her hand, bringing it to his chest to let her feel his heart beating. "Please, Cathy, we were good together. Let's try this again, for the children's sake?"

She shook her head. "Gary—"

"No! No, just think about it. You, me, Millie, and Jack. In this house, or somewhere else, if you want. We can sell up here and move someplace better, somewhere foreign. Start again, as a family."

His eyes bored into hers as he edged closer, laying his heart on the line, willing her to agree with him.

"I love you, Cathy," he said again, the lump growing bigger in his throat. "Always have and always will. Give us another chance." He lifted his hand up to touch her face, cupping her cheek as he leaned in to kiss her.

"Gary…I'm pregnant."

He froze on the spot, inches from her face, all his plans collapsing into his gut. "Ah, fuck it, anyway!"

22nd April

Tuesday

With the children at Gary's, Cathy and Sam made the most of their free time together. Being able to speak freely about the baby was something they couldn't do with two sets of inquisitive ears nearby. When it came to finding out a secret, Millie and Jack had superpowers, so it was best to discuss things when they weren't around.

They went for a drive, and stopped in at Jack Whites Inn for some pub grub. Cathy sipped spring water, while Sam enjoyed a pint of Guinness with his lunch.

"You just can't beat a pint of the black stuff," he said, wiping the frothy head off his lips.

She thumbed out the waistband on her jeans, trying to give her stomach room to expand after the delicious food. "I'm fit to burst."

"It won't be long before you're wearing those big flowing maternity frocks," Sam said, rubbing his own washboard abs.

She laughed. "Who even says *frock* anymore? What century are you from?"

His cheeks reddened and he waved her away. "Ah, you know what I mean. Those long maxi-dresses, with plenty of room for your growing bump." He signalled to the waiter for the bill.

"Firstly," she said, determined to put him straight on a few things, "it will be months before I'll need to give up my jeans. I'm only seven weeks gone so the baby won't be showing for a while yet." She rested her forearms on the table and fixed him with hard eye-contact. "And secondly, under no circumstances will I be wearing any sort of maternity frock, maxi-dress, or otherwise."

He reached across the table and rubbed her hand.

She smiled at his touch and patted the back of his hand. "I prefer the leggings and baggy t-shirt look, actually. Much more comfortable and practical. That outfit is better than any of those flowy things, with their yards of material. It's an accident waiting to happen, and they're ridiculously expensive, if you ask me. A few pairs of leggings and a handful of extra-large t-shirts, of varying colours, will do me just fine. No need to waste money on expensive, specialist clothes that never see the light of day again once the baby is born."

Sam squeezed her hand between both of his. "Please don't be worrying about money, Cathy. I'm here for you now and I want to look after you, do the best for you, and make sure you have all that your heart desires."

"I know," she said, leaning over and kissing him, "but you have to remember something, Sam – I've had to budget, quite strictly, for the past few years and, if nothing else, it's made me realise how much money I've wasted on frivolous things, stuff I

189

didn't really need or want, but thought I should buy just because I could."

The lounge girl brought the bill and Sam paid it with his card, leaving a generous tip on the side plate.

"I don't need fancy maternity clothes, Sam," Cathy continued, lifting her bag off the floor. Sam was wonderful, but sometimes he just didn't see the obvious. "Where do you think I'd be wearing them, anyway? A posh frock for the school run? Designer trousers, teamed with that speciality blouse, for sitting in a cold drama hall or stinky swimming pool?"

He lifted both hands, palms out. "Okay, I'll concede to you not needing maternity clothes, but you have to understand that I want you to share this with me, financially, emotionally, and physically." He moved around the small table and sat beside her. "Anything you need, I'll get it for you. Anything you want to talk about, good or bad, I'll be here, listening." He looked straight into her eyes, and she could see that he was inviting her to let him in. "When you're tired and hormonal, with swollen ankles and haemorrhoids, I'll be there to massage your feet and—"

"What are you going to do, Sam?" she asked, laughing out loud. "Are you going to tend to my piles?" She touched his knee, feeling bad for laughing when he was trying so hard to have a moment. "I think that's taking the expectant-daddy role a bit too far, don't you?"

He leaned back, his eyes closed and a pained look of mortification on his face. "Yeah, yeah, okay, I get it. But you know what I mean, don't you? I won't actually tend to your…thingies, but I will go and buy you the cream." He took a long slug of his pint and wiped his top lip clean. "You can rub it in yourself," he said, a little too loudly, causing the family eating dinner two tables up to stare.

"Oh, Jesus." Cathy's face burned.

Sam threw a megawatt smile in their direction, apologising for mentioning such things when they were eating their dinner. "But it's okay," he said, nodding at Cathy, "she's pregnant."

She shook her head in disbelief. *How can I bring this conversation back to some sort of normality?* "Sam, I wanted to talk about something you said the other day."

"Go ahead," he said, focusing on her again.

"Well, you were talking about Sorcha, and about you moving back to Ireland." She was unsure how to approach the subject without causing him more hurt. But he needed to hear the truth, as she saw it. "All this stuff with Sorcha – the expensive trainers, the concert, and all the other malarkey – I think she's playing you. All right, I'm only reading between the lines, and going by what you've told me, but both Sorcha and her mother seem to be in this together. Taking advantage."

"I know what you're saying," he said, peeling the surface off a beer mat on the table. He kept his eyes averted, almost as if he was afraid to tackle the subject with her, or embarrassed that others in the pub might hear.

"Come on, Sam, we're here for each other, aren't we?"

"Of course, of course." He glanced around and sighed, then motioned towards the door. Cathy was comfortable at the table, but realised that he wanted to speak more privately, and so followed him out to the car.

He reached the sleek black BMW first, flicked off the alarm with the press of a button, then turned to Cathy with a tortured look on his face. "When I went looking for Sorcha, I couldn't believe I'd been given a second chance to be a father. That time when Sinead admitted she didn't lose the baby, that I actually had an nine-year-old daughter living in London, I knew that if I fucked it up, I might never get the chance to do it again."

With the door open, he braced his hands on the roof of the car. "You saw how crazy I was back then. I needed to right the wrong I didn't even know I'd made."

Cathy watched his torment from a few steps away, letting him speak freely, no matter how difficult it was for her to hear.

"The one thing I knew for certain was that I needed to meet Sorcha, in person, to explain that I hadn't been given the option of knowing her for all those years. Sinead made that decision for me, years ago, and now it was up to me to do what I could to right the matter."

Cathy's heart went out to him. She hated reminding him of that awful time, but there was no getting away from what had been done, or said. "You had hard decisions to make, involving lots of people. I understand all that. Really, I do, but that's not my point."

"I know what your point is," he responded, his tone sharp.

"Do not snap at me, Sam O'Keefe. I'm only bringing this up because I don't want you turning around in ten years' time and blaming me for making you move back to Ireland. Ever since we found out about this baby, it's been difficult to know how you really feel about moving back here. It feels like you think it can be only one way or the other – like you have to give Sorcha up because of me. I can't let you think like that." She closed the gap between them and forced him to turn around and look directly at her.

"I'm putting no pressure on you, Sam. You know that because we've been over this a hundred times already, but I need you to promise me that you don't feel you're giving your daughter up because of me."

"I'm not giving her up," he said, running his hands through his hair. "And she knows that." He reached out and took her hand, easing her towards him. "I love you, Cathy." He kissed her hand, intertwined with his. "Believe me, I know I'm being soft with Sorcha. And I fully realise she's playing me." He took a deep breath and shrugged. "She barely batted an eyelid and didn't give a damn when I told her I was moving back here. All she wanted was the free trip away with her friends. But *I* needed to feel that I'm not abandoning her. I needed to clear my conscious."

"To be honest, I've spent the last six months getting to know her and her family, and even if you weren't pregnant, I think I'd have moved back soon, anyway."

Cathy remained silent, listening as he opened up, laying his feelings bare for her, for them.

"Sorcha isn't how I expected her to be. I don't know why, with a biological mother like Sinead, but I had visions of a princess bubble-gum – a sweet little girl. Instead, she's a spoilt brat with a serious attitude problem." He looked around the half-empty car park, almost like he was nervous to admit his true feelings to anyone, even Cathy.

"Go on, Sam," she said, squeezing his hand, not wanting him to stop now.

He lowered his gaze and nodded. "I'm not leaving her completely. She's still my daughter, no matter what type of little tyrant she grows up to be, but I'm happy to leave the day-to-day stuff to Aoife and Bill. They've raised her their way, and while they're willing to live with how she turns out, I'm not sure I can – not up close, anyway. The three of them know I never expected to be a permanent fixture on-site, so to speak, and I'm happy to take a backseat now and see where the road takes us."

Tears stung Cathy's eyes. Sam had opened up so completely, laying his biggest fears and regrets out on the table. "Are you sure? I mean, really sure? Is this definitely what you want?"

He looked at her, the tension gone from his face and shoulders. "Cathy, how many times do I have to say it? I love you. I'm over the moon about this baby. I'm back, with you, and whether you like it or not, I'm here to stay."

She let out the breath she'd been holding, her doubts finally banished. He was her man, and she loved and trusted him with all her heart. Nobody was going to affect that. If there was one person she was going to keep a close eye on, it was his scheming diva daughter – Sorcha.

23rd April

Wednesday

It had been almost a week since Byron had left Cathy sitting in the café, too upset to explain properly or even speak to her friend about what was really bothering her. She'd ignored almost daily attempts from Cathy to contact her, knowing she was being childish, but unable to help herself.

Her work was suffering as well. She couldn't concentrate, muddling through each eight-hour day, her only relief when the clock hit five p.m.

Tom was waiting outside to collect her, and that brought a welcome smile as she exited the front door of her office building. Having worked two night shifts this week, he was due time off and they planned to spend it on wedding preparations.

"Hey, babe," he said, his eyes lighting up as she approached him.

"Oh, am I glad to see you, my hunky fireman." She stretched on tip-toes to reach his mouth with hers, not caring one dot about the public display of affection or that her skirt now rode up almost to her bottom. Tom caressed the smooth skin of her thigh, before chuckling and tugging her skirt back down.

"So, what's the plan for tonight?" he asked, clasping her hand and setting off towards his car.

"Well, I was thinking we might treat ourselves to a nice Indian takeaway."

"Ooh, I like the sound of that."

"Open a bottle of wine…"

"Excellent," he said, his arm now around her shoulders.

"And then, maybe we can get a jumpstart on the wedding invitations? I picked them up today." She held up a plastic carrier bag.

"Ah, Byron, seriously? I thought we were gonna have some hot fun tonight."

She laughed at the little lost-boy look he used when she didn't readily agree to sex morning, noon, and night. "Maybe later," she conceded, a thrilling shiver running down her spine as he caressed the back of her neck. "But first, food, wine, and invitations."

"All right, but you'd better do the writing and all the fancy bits and pieces. I'll stuff the envelopes and lick the stamps. Job done."

She laughed again and elbowed him. "You know I bought sticky stamps on a roll, you brat, so you got a lucky break there – no licking for you. Well, not until later." She winked and squeezed his thick bicep. "And remember, we chose the scrolls, so the pages need to be rolled, tied neatly with little ribbons, then placed in their own cardboard tube. All you need to do then is seal each one with wax, stamp it with our personalized seal, and fix the address label and postage stamp neatly in place."

Tom groaned, squeezing his eyes shut as he unlocked the car. "Here was me thinking I was getting off lightly, but it looks like I'll be doing most of the donkey work. All you have to do is scribble a few names on the top of the page and the rest is up to me."

As they eased out into the line of rush-hour traffic, Byron couldn't help smiling as Tom grumbled on about ribbons and wax seals, loving him even more when he actually suggested they could spray the scrolls with her favourite perfume. They kept the friendly banter up all the way home, talking about this and that, her day and his, until finally Tom's face turned serious.

"Look, babe, I'm just going to come right out and say this, all right? And don't freak out."

She froze, imagining the worst. "You cancelled the music for the church, didn't you?" She planted a hand on her forehead. "I knew your mother didn't approve of violins in the church. Did she make you cancel it? Did she?"

Tom shook his head, his half-smile battling with something deeper, more worrisome. "It's nothing to do with the church. Just listen."

Her nerves weren't up for this – there was way too much going on. "Come on, spit it out. What did you do?" She looked at him, sensing that this really was serious.

"I...spoke to Cathy today."

She slapped the dash. "Ah, Tom!"

"Look, honey, she's really upset, and you're really upset, so you need to talk to her to get this sorted once and for all."

"I—"

"No, Byron, you've got to listen to me. It's gone way too far."

"But I—"

"I'm serious, it's not—"

"Jesus, Tom, will you let me get a word in edgeways?"

He glanced at her, his mouth open. "Okay, go ahead."

"I know what you're saying," she said, closing her eyes and shaking her head, feeling like the biggest idiot in the world. "I've been such a stubborn fool, I've let it go too long and now I don't know what to say, or how to make contact – the first move."

"Exactly. That's why I invited her up to the house this evening, so the two of you can talk."

Her stomach jumped and she whipped around to be met by his straight face. He wasn't joking. "You're serious?" She wrung her hands together as she thought about the prospect of facing her best friend, and how unfair she'd been – how childish.

"Oh, Tom, I've been such an idiot. I'm terrified, but you're right, it's better to clear the air. I'll tell her exactly how I feel."

199

"No need to. I already did."

"Eh, what exactly did you say?" The words come out almost in a whisper.

"That you thought it was very bad timing, her getting pregnant, right before our wedding, and that you were jealous of all the attention she'd be getting, and that she was stealing your thunder."

Byron gasped, hardly able to believe he'd told her all that. He'd made her out to be a spoilt diva, having a tantrum and throwing her toys out of the pram.

"You didn't actually tell her that, did you?" she asked, once she could talk again, speaking slowly and quietly, determined not to lose her rag. "Please tell me you're messing."

He kept one eye on the road, breaking into a big grin. "Well, I didn't completely throw you under the bus and let the whole world know how crazy you really are. And, anyway, Cathy already knows you're nuts, and she loves you for it, just like me."

His grin turned into a broad smile as he swung the car into a free space outside their townhouse. Cathy's car was already there, a few spaces away. She climbed out as Tom parked.

Byron could see how nervous she was, but also how tired and worn out she looked. Concern washed over her and she got out and ran, reaching out when they met, pulling her into a tight embrace, not wanting to let go.

"I'm so sorry, Cathy. I've been stupid and childish." Tears welled as she realised how much she'd missed her friend, and how stupid and idiotic she'd been not speaking to her for the past week.

Cathy returned the hug, so hard Byron thought she would crack.

"Tom explained it all to me." She released her hold and fished in her pocket and took a tissue out. "I'm sorry, Byron. I know this baby is bad timing, but I didn't do it on purpose. I swear I didn't. I would never do anything to take even one second of happiness away from you. Please believe that."

Byron let the tears flow, not bothering to mop them up, because she knew there was plenty still to come. "Oh, Cathy, I know you didn't get pregnant on purpose. And so what if you did? What difference does it make?" She wiped her eyes with the heel of each hand, feeling guiltier than ever. How could she have thought Cathy had planned this in order take away from her wedding day? *Such a fool.*

Cathy offered her a clean tissue. "I haven't even told my parents yet, or Sam's. Nobody else knows, and that's the way it's going to stay for another few months. The spotlight will be firmly focused on you. No distraction, whatsoever."

Byron couldn't believe how understanding Cathy was being. "Look at the way I've acted. I've been such a nutcase over this wedding, I couldn't even stop for one minute and be happy for you. My reaction to your wonderful news is unforgivable." She took a shuddering breath and held her best friend's hand. "Your pregnancy is both wonderful and terrifying, and I'm afraid I took the whole bridezilla reaction a step too far. I'm so, so sorry. Please forgive me?"

Cathy smiled through the tears. "Nothing to forgive, By." She squeezed her hand. "Once Tom told me what was going on, I totally understood why you reacted like you did. I don't blame you. To be honest, I'd be upset, too, if someone tried to upstage me on my wedding day. In fact, if it was anyone pulling this pregnancy stunt like I did, I'd be giving out to them myself, on your behalf, for ruining your day."

With fresh tears rolling down her cheeks, Bryon leaned back and stared at her friend. "You're not ruining my day. Please don't think that. This is your life, your baby, and it was selfish of me to think that it would affect me in any other way than being concerned and delight for you, and wishing you a healthy pregnancy and a safe delivery nine months down the road." She wiped her runny nose with the soaked tissue. "I'm so glad you're here, Cathy." She pulled her in for another hug. "I've missed you."

I've missed you, too," Cathy said, burying her face in Bryon's shoulder.

"Okay, now that's all over," Tom called from where he'd been standing behind them, "I'm going for a pint."

"What?" Byron turned herself and Cathy around to face her fiancé.

Tom held up his phone. "I've ordered a takeaway for you both. It should be here in a minute. Oh, and Cathy?"

"Yeah?" She stood linking Byron, both of them smiling.

"Byron has a great job for you. It involves ribbons and tubes, and she thinks you'd be great at it. Don't you, By?" He chuckled and winked.

Byron went to kiss Tom. She stretched up to his ear, her lips touching his skin. "I love you, my hunky fireman. Thank you."

Byron felts his arms wrap around her waist, pulling her up against him.

"Don't mention it, Kiddo. It's my job." He winked at Cathy. "I'm a pro at rescuing people from themselves and sorting out catfights."

Cathy rolled her eyes, while Byron stared, wide-eyed at his face.

"And God help me," he continued, "I've had enough practice with you lot. Between you, Cathy, and Annabel, you'd certainly keep us good men on our toes." He leaned down and kissed the tip of Byron's nose.

Heat rushed into her face and she grinned up at him. "And that's the way it's supposed to be." She returned the kiss, but to his mouth instead, nibbling on his lower lip. "Perhaps if you stay for some dinner," she said, keeping her voice low, "and then go for your pint, maybe when you get back, I'll be in just the right mood to show you my appreciation for all your…thoughtfulness."

"Erm, I'll wait over here, guys," Cathy said, giggling as she walked up to the front door.

Tom looked at Byron through lust-filled eyes. "Will you wear that black lacy thing you got last month?" He bent to kiss her again.

"Mmm…maybe I'll be wearing nothing at all."

"Now you're talking," he said. Byron kissed him, deep and hard, giving him a preview of what he could expect later.

24th April

Thursday

Rain hopped off the ground as Millie and Jack looked out the living-room window.

"Aw, Mammy, we can't go out to play," Millie said, groaning in unison with her brother.

Cathy's bones ached – she was exhausted, and even though she felt better after clearing the air with Byron, she still struggled with the early pregnancy symptoms. Her morning sickness, at least, had eased, and she'd stopped being sick every day, now only feeling the nausea return when she smelled something fishy or strongly scented. However, the coma-inducing tiredness was difficult to deal with when she had two bored twins to entertain.

"Okay, lads, get your socks and shoes on." She endeavoured, for their sake, to instil a bit of excitement into her voice. "We're going to Kidzone."

The children erupted into excited jumps and leaps, racing out to the hall.

"Kidzone is the best place ever," Millie said as she sorted her right shoe from her left.

"I love the football pitch," Jack said, unable to find a matching pair of runners, so pulled on a pair of wellingtons instead.

"You always play football," Millie complained. "You should try the climbing frame for a change, and the wibbly-wobbly bridge. They're the best things there and you never go on them."

Jack looked wary, as if he was being challenged to give up his football, but then he just shrugged. "Okay, I'll give it a go, but if I don't enjoy myself, it's all your fault."

Millie assured him she would never steer him wrong when it came to playing, and went off to find a hat, scarf, and gloves.

Cathy had to smile at them. She went into the kitchen and rang Sam, to chat to him briefly before they left.

"Hey, it's lashing down here. We're heading off to Kidzone. How are you?" She could hear a lot of noise in the background, which quietened as she waited for him to answer.

"It's not going well here at all," he said, his voice edged with frustration, making her worry he'd taken on too much.

His family owned a chain of pubs and clubs around Dublin, but lately they'd taken over three new premises with the intention of expanding the O'Keefe brand outside the Pale, otherwise known as Dublin. Since his return, Sam had made himself available as project manager, overseeing the refurbishment of two pubs and a total review of procedures and staff at the new club in Galway.

Today, he was in Celbridge, a village just outside Dublin.

"It seems like our contractors are more interested in doing a quick job badly, than a good job properly." He went on to explain how already that morning he'd waited two hours for the carpenter to arrive, only to discover the materials they were using were of an inferior quality to the ones he'd requested. "These guys thought they could get away with using shabby cut-offs left over from a previous job." His voice rose as his anger intensified. "I'm not having it, Cathy. It's one thing trying to save a few quid here and there. We all do that. But this contract is worth hundreds of thousands, and I want the job done right."

Cathy nearly choked. *Hundreds of thousands?* She regained her composure and tried to soothe him by agreeing wholeheartedly with what he was saying. "Well, of course you do, Sam. Especially when you're paying out money like that."

"It's not my money," he said. "We have investors involved, and there's no way I'm going to let this renovation continue unless these guys start acting like professionals and do the job properly."

"I agree," she said again, not sure what else to say.

He groaned. "So that's my nightmare for today. Not so bad now that you've called. It's nice to hear your voice, sweet lady. How are you getting on? Do you miss me?"

"Do you know something funny?" She was almost afraid to say it in case she came across as desperate and needy. "I miss you more since you moved back to Ireland, and you leave me for eight or nine hours a day instead of weeks. I hate you leaving in the mornings, and can't wait for you to come home. Does that sound crazy?"

"I know exactly what you mean," he said. "It's like I'm so close, but it could be a million miles away. When I was in London, I knew I couldn't just jump in the car and drive home to you. It was kind of easier. But now, I think of nothing except you, all day long, wondering if anyone would notice if I left and drove home at one hundred miles an hour to meet you for a quickie."

She laughed. "You're so sweet, Sam O'Keefe. What a lovely way to speak to the mother of your unborn child." Then her laughter turned to tears, and she had to catch her breath as sobs queued to escape out of her mouth.

"What's wrong, Cathy?" he asked, his voice panicky. "Why are you crying?"

"I don't know," she blubbered, unable to stem the flow.

"It must be something. Please tell me."

She sniffed and cleared her nose, struggling to form a coherent sentence which, in her current state, wasn't easy. "It's just, well, you're being so nice to me." More sobs followed.

He chuckled. "Aren't I always nice to you?"

"I know," she said, "that's why I'm crying. Oh, don't mind me, Sam – I'm all hormonal."

"I don't care," he replied, "you're my woman, and that's all that counts."

She sniffled and coughed. "Yes, I am, and you're right, and you're so good to say that with me blubbering down the line to you."

"And you deserve the sun, moon, and stars, every single morning when you wake up," he said, "and to be tucked in like a princess every single night."

Tears ran down her cheeks as she smiled, picturing him in front of her saying those words to her face. His chivalry, not allowing her to fail at anything. He would always be there to protect her.

"Hey, what happens when I get fat and floppy and grumpy?" she asked, showing him she was over the worst of it and was now ready to play.

"Ah, sure that won't matter to me. You're already floppy and grumpy, so it's no biggie having to deal with a fatty as well."

She couldn't help but laugh, feeling much better than five minutes ago.

"I promise to love you, no matter which parts of you droop, or if the middle-age spread wreaks havoc with your belly. It won't matter to me, no way."

She took a deep breath and wiped her nose. One thing was for sure, she'd need to stock up on tissues over the next few months, if the past few days were anything to go by.

"Are you okay now?" Sam asked.

"Yes, I'm much better now. Thanks to you."

"No problem, but look, Cathy, I have to go. Is that okay?"

"Of course," she answered. "I'll be fine, it's just the hormones. Anyway, how much crying can you really do in the middle of a padded play area, with screaming kids everywhere, and a line of stressed-out mothers to talk to?"

"Okay, I'll ring you later, or you ring me, if you need anything. I love you. Bye."

"Bye, Sam, I'll talk to you soon. Love you, too."

***

In Kidzone, Cathy bought a cup of tea and sat at the last empty table. She watched as Millie and Jack raced through the soft play area, glad to see them getting a chance to really enjoy themselves. They needed to stretch their legs. Two weeks' Easter holidays was a long time for children to deal with. They were so used to the routine provided by the school, that anything longer than three days away had them bored and irritable, looking for things to do, especially when it was raining.

Jack ran towards her, his face red with exertion, stripping off his zipped jumper as he approached. "This is great, Mam." He panted as he reached for his bottle of water. "Millie was right about the climbing frame. It's brilliant, and the wibbly-wobbly bridge is now my second-favourite thing, after football."

He ran off again, his chair quickly filled by another mother, Roisin, who Cathy knew from school.

"How are you, Roisin?" she asked, smiling. "How are the Easter holidays going?"

"Don't talk to me, Cathy." She released her infant baby from the sling strapped to her chest.

Before Cathy could blink, Roisin pulled up her shirt, exposing her right breast to the whole room, then latched the baby on with the practiced moves of a pro.

Even though she supported women who chose to breastfeed, she always felt uncomfortable when a boob was whipped out, right in front of her. She never knew where to look, and wondered what the correct protocol for spectators in the breastfeeding arena was.

"You have your hands full there." She made a point of keeping her eyes focused on Roisin's face.

Roisin smiled. "Ah, it's not so bad." She clucked the baby under the chin, smiling down at his innocent face, oblivious to the stares she was receiving from some of the other adults.

As Cathy glanced around, she couldn't help feeling bad for her. She was doing nothing wrong. Breastfeeding was the most natural thing in the world, and Roisin didn't deserve the looks of disgust that were coming her way.

An anger sparked in Cathy. She sent dirty looks back in their direction as she listened to Roisin talk freely about how her eldest son, Stevie, was finding it tough to accept his new sibling as not a plaything, but a real life person. "I've found him trying to climb into the cot a few times, and he seems to have regressed, asking for his soother and his blankie. I even caught him trying to latch on here once, when this little fella was taking a break."

Cathy paled, picturing a two-month old baby suckling on one side, while his brother joined him for a quick snack on the other.

Thankfully, Millie ran over, wanting to go to the bathroom. She wasted no time in getting up.

"Nice seeing you, Cathy," Roisin said. Her baby finished feeding and she fixed herself and placed him back in the chest sling.

"Yes, you too," Cathy said, leaning forward to pat the baby's head, rubbing the downy fluff on the folds of his neck. "Best of luck with him. He's beautiful."

"Ah, thanks. Good luck to you, too."

Cathy nodded and kept going, sure she'd misheard. How could Roisin know she was pregnant? She wasn't showing and she certainly wasn't glowing. Maybe the woman had some sort of sixth sense. After recently given birth herself, could she zone in on others who were in the womanly way?

She waited outside the toilet cubicle for Millie to finish. A cramping pain gripped her lower back, knocking the air out of her before it disappeared. *What the hell was that?* She grabbed the sink while she caught her breath. The pain came again, not as intense this time, but still bad enough to make her worry.

She pulled out her phone and speed-dialled Sam.

"Sam?" She kept her voice low, not wanting Millie to hear. "Sam, something's not right. I think there's something wrong with the baby. I'm scared, Sam."

"Calm down. What happened?" he asked quickly. She told him of the searing pain that had almost doubled her over and then the small cramp-like pains that were coming and going.

"I'm sure it's nothing to worry about, Cathy. It sounds like implantation cramps." This shocked her into silence. "I read about it last night in that pregnancy book you have. It's normal at this stage."

"Well, it doesn't feel normal," she bit out between clenched teeth. "It feels like there's something wrong."

"Okay, sorry, sorry, you're right. You know your own body better than anyone." He coughed. "Em…are there any other symptoms?"

"No, I don't think so. It just happened." Millie emerged from the cubicle and went to wash her hands. Cathy put her hand over the phone's mouthpiece and told her to go quickly and get her brother.

"I'm going home, Sam. I'm frightened. I don't think this is right."

"I'm on my way," he said, "I'll be there within the hour. Do you think you're okay to drive?"

"Yes, I think so," she answered, moving to look for the children. She spotted them at the shoe-collection point. Both had already donned their coats and scarves, and Millie was helping Jack put on his boots.

"Okay, drive carefully, get yourself and the kids home. Put a DVD on for them and get into bed, okay?"

She gestured for the children to follow her to the exit gate. As she spoke to Sam, she heard his car start and the screech of tyres as he left the pub.

"Okay, I'm leaving now, Sam. I'll be home in five minutes. I'll be okay, I think, the pain is starting to ease a bit." She strapped the children into the car.

"I'll be with you soon. Hang on, I'm on my way." He disconnected, and she started the engine and drove slowly back to her house.

She spoke calmly to Millie and Jack all the way home, not so much for them, but to keep things steady for herself. The last thing she wanted was to go into panic-mode. "Mammy's not feeling well," she said, making eye-contact in her rear-view mirror, "so

214

we're going to go upstairs and snuggle in my bed, and watch a DVD."

"What's wrong with you?" Jack asked.

"I just have a little headache, so you and Millie need to be really quiet, okay?" They nodded back at her and she thanked God for allowing her to be their mammy. They really were the best in the world.

Ten minutes later, she loaded a Disney DVD into the player and squeezed between her two little angels already snuggled on the bed. A dull ache pulsed in her lower back, and she tried to ignore the obvious warning signs. She wrapped her arms around Millie and Jack, hugging them tight as she waited for Sam, closing her eyes and praying she wasn't experiencing what she really feared was happening – a miscarriage.

25th April

Friday

Cathy's eyes fluttered open at the heat of a hand holding hers. The room was too bright and she had to shield her eyes, blinking against the glare. Sam. Her breath caught when she realised they were in a hospital room, surrounded by beeping machines and monitors.

He sat on the side of the bed and took her in his arms. "Everything is going to be okay," he whispered, rocking her back and forth. "You're okay. I promise."

She buried her face against the warmth of his neck, her silence broken by an involuntary sob. "The baby? Sam, how's the baby?"

"Baby is fine," he said, leaning back and smiling. "You had a bleed last night, but the doctors were able to stop it. Do you not remember?"

She touched her forehead and blinked as everything came back. "Yes, yes, I remember. Is Mam still with the twins?"

"Yep, fair play to her. The poor woman couldn't have received shorter notice to drop everything and run. She's worried sick about you, but you know the twins are in safe hands with her."

The door opened and a woman walked in. Cathy remembered her – the doctor who'd looked after her when she'd come in cramped up and bleeding.

"Hello, Cathy. Good to see you're awake."

"Hi, Doctor. Sam was filling me in."

She smiled. "Good, then you know everything is just fine."

Cathy caught something in the doctor's eyes. She looked to Sam, then back again. The doctor frowned.

"I'm sorry, Doctor," Sam said, "I didn't get a chance to…"

"That's okay." She smiled again, checking Cathy's chart. "You gave us a bit of a fright, but once we found the reason for your bleed, the problem became obvious, and easily sorted."

"The reason?" Her face went cold at the memory of rushing in with the fear that her bleed meant she was losing the baby. "I remember there were doctors and nurses running everywhere."

"Yes, but that's how we work here. It looks chaotic, but everyone knows their place." She smiled that wonderful smile again. "So, once we took the ruptured polyp off the lining of your womb, Baby now has all the room he or she needs to grow."

Cathy took a deep breath and let out a long sigh. She laid both hands on her tummy. "A polyp. A feckin' polyp." She looked up. "So everything is going to be okay?"

"I see no reason why not. The polyp and Baby were in direct competition. The polyp lost out, and Baby is still there, showing a steady heartbeat."

Tears came to Cathy's eyes when she recalled the nurse pointing out her little baby on the monitor, still alive despite all the trauma surrounding it.

"Okay," the doctor said, placing the chart back on the end of the bed, "we'll bring you some tea and toast, but then I want you to have a rest. After that, we'll see how you are."

Cathy had to smile when Sam took the doctor's hand and thanked her profusely, so much the doctor actually blushed.

When they were alone, Sam held her. "Believe in miracles, Cathy, because it's the biggest miracle of all that your body managed to hold onto our baby. It just shows how strong you are. How strong both of you are."

"You're my strength, Sam O'Keefe. Once you're in my life, I know everything will be okay."

***

Later, when she awoke from a restful sleep, a nurse came in to check her stats. "How are you feeling, pet?" she asked, smiling kindly in the only way nurses can. "You gave everyone a pretty good scare last night."

"I know," Cathy said. "I'm still a bit shaky, to be honest, but so relieved that everything is okay."

"I know Doctor McCoy told you that rest is important, so you need to listen to her. Your body got an awful shock, you know. It needs time to recover." She filled a glass with water and placed it on the locker beside the bed. "The good news is your vitals are good, and I've been reliably informed that you're free to go whenever you feel up to it."

Cathy looked at Sam, who was nearly crying. "I want to go home, Sam, to my own bed, to my children. I can rest there."

"Okay then, missy," the nurse said, moving to the door, "I'll go get your discharge papers sorted. You can sign them at reception. We don't want to see you back here until Baby's good and ready to enter the world, on schedule, covered in everything good your birth canal has to offer. Understood?" Her stern look was shattered by a gleaming smile. Then she was gone.

Cathy laughed out loud at the look of horror on Sam's face.

He shook his head, as if releasing himself of images men shouldn't see. "Seriously, did she need to be so graphic?"

"Ah, she was only having a laugh. Just doing her job."

"Yeah, but still," he said, helping her out of the bed, "I'm not sure I'm able for the more gory part of this deal."

She laid her hand on his chest. "God love you, Sam. When this baby really does make an appearance, you'll see quick enough how polite conversation and dignity goes flying out the window. You'll not believe some of the questions I'll be asked. I'm serious, you'd better be prepared for it."

"Jesus," he groaned, helping her get dressed, then stood straight and stuck his chest out. "I won't let you down, Cathy Byrne. I mean that. I'll just need to get my head around a few things first."

She hugged him. "I have complete faith in you, Sam. Don't ever doubt that."

He took her bag and led her out into the corridor. When they passed the hospital chapel, he knocked twice on the wooden door. Cathy smiled. "Didn't take you for the superstitious type."

"Hey, I'm just sending my thanks to the big fella upstairs. I'll do my best to protect you, but I can do with some help from the man up above as well."

26th April

Saturday

"Are you listening to me, Cathy?" Annabel asked, pressing the phone into her cheek, almost as if it would get her closer. "You're to take it easy. I know everybody's probably saying it to you, and you're no doubt sick of hearing it, but you have to understand that we're all worried about you, chicken."

"I know," Cathy said. "I will."

"And why didn't you tell anyone you were feeling bad?" Annabel did her best not to sound as if she was scolding her friend.

"It all happened so fast, Annabel. I rang Sam, and thank God he got home when he did, because I dread to think what could have happened if I'd left it any longer."

"Well, you're right about that, but will you just remember in future that we're all here for you? I know Sam is like an overprotective mama bear with you at the moment, but if you need anything at all, Byron and I are always just a phone call away."

"But, Annabel, you guys are so busy with your own lives. Byron is up to her tonsils with the wedding, and you just got Jean Luc back into the country. Neither of you need me ringing complaining about my aches and pains."

"Sweet Jesus," Annabel nearly shouted, biting back her frustration. "Cathy, you nearly lost your baby. This was one of those times you needed to use your head and think, 'Okay, I'm in trouble, who can I ring to get to me quickly? Who's the closest?'"

She pinched the bridge of her nose just thinking of what might have happened if Sam hadn't been there to help. "Never, ever be afraid to ring me or Byron when you're in trouble. Sam was an hour away. I could have been with you in twenty minutes. I probably wouldn't have done anything differently, but at least you wouldn't have been on your own with the children, petrified out of your skin."

"I know you're here for me," Cathy said, her voice almost a whisper. "I just panicked. I wasn't thinking straight. But don't worry, I won't be doing any more running around. In fact, I think Sam has both of you earmarked for a bit of Cathy-sitting over the next few weeks."

Annabel sat up. "Ooh, sounds like a plan. You, me, and Byron relaxing and taking it easy. I like the sound of that. Maybe he can treat us all to a mini Spa break, strictly for medicinal purposes, I mean."

They chatted for a while longer, before Annabel had to go. "Mind yourself, Cathy. I'll ring you tomorrow, okay?"

"Look forward to it. And please don't worry, I'm fine."

"Don't you dare lift a finger, Cathy Byrne. Let Sam organise things. The children are at Gary's today and tomorrow, right?"

"Yes."

"Okay, so you rest, sleep, and let your body recover. I'll give you a call tomorrow."

"Thanks, Annabel."

"For what?"

"For being you. For being my friend. I love you. See you soon, bye."

***

Annabel refilled her glass with wine from the open bottle in the fridge. *God, poor Cathy. The poor thing.* She wrapped her arms around her waist, comforting herself as she wished she could comfort her friend.

Jean Luc arrived, laden down with bags from a little French delicatessen a few streets away. He put the food on the counter before pulling Annabel into his harms, kissing each cheek twice.

She snuggled her face into the crook of his neck, savouring the warmth and strength in his embrace.

"I was just speaking with Cathy," she said, snuggling in closer.

Jean Luc stroked the back of her head, letting his fingers run through her silky red curls. "How is she today?"

"Much better. Sam has her wrapped in cotton wool and won't let her move an inch." Annabel knew she'd do the same in Sam's position, even if it drove Cathy crazy. "I'll give her a ring again tomorrow and see when it suits to visit. She needs her rest, but she also needs to know her friends are there for her."

"Good plan," Jean Luc said. "I am glad to hear she is doing better. You were so worried about her, as was I. It is a precious gift she is carrying, the little baby. She has good friends. You and Byron, as well as Sam, all ready for her to lean on, no?"

"That's exactly what I said to her." She eased out of his arms and moved to the kitchen to unpack the groceries. "She needs to start letting people in. Asking for help. When you're not feeling well, you should talk about it, not bury it. A problem shared is a problem halved, you know?"

Jean Luc followed her into the small kitchen. "And is that how it is with you?"

"What about me?" she asked, trying to avoid the conversation she suspected was coming by burying her head in the fridge.

"I tried to speak with you about this a few times. You continue to change the subject." He moved over to her and rested his hands on her shoulders. "There is a terrible weight on these beautiful shoulders." He kissed her ear. "I want to know how I can help."

"It's nothing." She sighed and leaned back against him. "It's just a bit of hassle I'm having with someone at work."

"Oh, yes, you spoke about this before, but I thought it was sorted. It all happened a few weeks ago, no?"

She didn't really want to talk, but knew by the look in his eyes that he wanted answers. Other times he'd broached the subject, she'd managed to steer the conversation in a different direction, or just shut him up by clamping her mouth over his in a passionate French kiss.

He was worried about her, and he deserved to know what was going on, but she'd spent years dealing with difficult situations on her own. Now she found it hard to lean on anyone else, to share the burden, even if it was by only talking it out and getting a weight off her chest. It had taken time for her to realise that Jean Luc wanted to be there for her, not only as a lover and a friend, but as someone to help when things got rough and worry kept her awake at night.

Forgetting about the food strewn on the kitchen counter, she filled a glass with wine for Jean Luc before leading him to the living-room area to sit down.

She sat beside him and thought it best to start from the beginning. "This girl in work has been a pain in the ass ever since she joined the company two months ago. She is inexperienced and lazy, and God only knows how she even got the job in the first place, never mind kept it."

The wine was gorgeous, but she fought back the urge to drink it down, simply wetting her lips with a sip. "I already told you how she almost got me fired a few weeks ago. She blamed me for not telling her a deadline was approaching, which meant she had to work extra hours to catch up. My job was on the line if she didn't finish that report but, thankfully, after a very stressful phone call the weekend I was in Kilkenny, she pulled out the finger and got the work done. By the skin of her teeth, I might add."

Jean Luc nodded. "I remember when you phoned me in Abu Dhabi to tell me all about it."

"Anyway, since then she's been blowing hot and cold with me. Going out of her way to find ways to trip me up, dumping shitty lawsuit files on my desk, spinning me some cock and bull story about how they were now my responsibility, etc. She tried everything to get me back for the bollocking I gave her on the phone that weekend."

"This woman sounds like an extreme case," Jean Luc said. "Her behaviour sounds very childish, but I don't see why you have to go along with it. Why can you not just say no?"

Annabel bit her lip, embarrassed to admit the reason Gemma had so much power over her. "I lost my patience with her one day and accused her of having lesbian sex with a senior manager."

Jean Luc snorted and raised an eyebrow. "Possibly not the best path to take."

"I know it was stupid, Jean Luc," she snapped.

"Is that it?" he asked. "Is that what has been bothering you all this time?"

"No, there's more," she admitted, giving in and knocking back the last of her wine. She stood up with the intention of getting a refill, but turned back. "She's threatening to make a complaint to HR if I don't do what she asks, and then to top it all off, my manager paid a visit to my office last week."

"Is this the senior manager you accused this other woman of having an affair with?" Jean Luc asked, his astonishment obvious as he leaned forward, awaiting her response.

"Yes, Ms Sandra Connolly. She's not someone you mess with, believe me." She shuddered at the thought and sat on a chair to prevent her legs shaking. "Sandra told me how she'd heard rumours that some of my clients had invested large amounts of money in return for inside information and sexual favours. Gemma, the bitch, made it all up and has been spreading barefaced lies about me and my work ethic."

Jean Luc paled as he looked at her.

Annabel noticed. "None of it's true, Jean Luc, please believe me. It's that fucking bitch, Gemma, stirring things up and trying to get me fired." She felt the now familiar quickening of her heartbeat and tried to keep her breathing under control before she fell apart. "Everyone from the top down is now watching every move I make. Apparently, all my clients are being reviewed, auditors brought in, and if there's one i not dotted or a t not crossed, I could lose my job and be in serious trouble, especially if they suspect inappropriate trading has occurred." She took a deep breath, relieved to have finally got it all off her chest. It terrified her that an auditor might not believe her word against Gemma's, and find a way of charging her with insider trading.

She clenched each side of her chair, turning her knuckles white as she struggled against the onset of a full-blown panic attack. Jean Luc knelt beside her and slipped a comforting arm around her shoulders

"I didn't do anything wrong," she said, her hands now covering her face to catch the sobs. "I've never acted with anything other than good faith where my clients are concerned. I go above and beyond what's expected of me to provide an excellent service, and I would never lower myself to a level where I offered favours, sexual or otherwise, in order to close a deal." She stood up and paced the room. "I'm damn good at my job, Jean Luc, and now this bitch, Gemma, has some sort of evil vendetta again me. My fucking name and reputation are being dragged through the mud and I could lose my job!"

Annabel noticed the look that passed across Jean Luc's face. It told her he was working through all the details.

"What is this Gemma's full name?" he asked, his voice quiet as he stared at the floor.

"Gemma O'Toole." She nearly spat out the words.

"Oui," he said, standing up, his fists clenched by his sides, "just as I thought."

Annabel stared at him, confused. "Do you know her?"

"Oui, I'm afraid I do." He pursed his lips, his body stiff as a poker. "Gemma O'Toole is a stalker, Annabel. She is the woman who has been hounding me for months, wanting me to fall in love with her. But I did not. I rejected her and now she is out for revenge."

Annabel collapsed onto the chair, her trembling legs unable to hold her any longer.

"She is hurting you to get to me, or perhaps trying to hurt me by getting at you." He checked his watch before taking out his phone, then knelt before Annabel, a look of real worry on his face.

"Stay away from her, Annabel. Gemma O'Toole is no ordinary woman scorned. She is dangerous and until we can get proof of harassment and threats she made against you, it is best to stay out of her way." He looked into her eyes, the intensity disturbing her in a way she hadn't expected. "She is after me, Annabel, and I think there is very little she will be afraid to try, until she finally gets the result she wants."

"Jesus Christ," Annabel cried, picking up her glass and flinging it against the wall. "All this torture I've been going through is because you rejected Gemma?" She couldn't believe it. "The fucking bitch needs locking up," she roared, anger burning into her eyes.

"Annabel, until we find out what she is at and how to stop her, you need to be careful. I must say it again, please stay away from her. I fear she is mentally unstable. There is no knowing what she might resort to if she is challenged. Gemma O'Toole is a loose cannon and you are not to put yourself in the firing line, no matter how much she taunts you. Agreed?"

Annabel looked away. There wasn't a chance she was letting this one go. Jean Luc pulled her to the couch, sitting down beside her.

"Perhaps if you do not believe my words," he said, "you will believe this." He unlocked his phone and scrolled through pictures until he found the one he wanted.

"Look." He held it up to her.

27th April

Sunday

Byron and Cathy sat wide-eyed and speechless as Annabel told the incredible story of Gemma O'Toole, psycho extraordinaire.

While Tom, Sam, and Jean Luc disappeared to the local pub, the girls made the most of their precious time together.

"Hurry up and tell us the rest," Cathy said when Annabel pleaded for a bathroom break. They'd drunk so much tea, she was sure her bladder would burst.

"Quickly," Cathy shouted up the stairs, "before Sam comes home and smothers me with cotton wool again."

"Don't be too hard on him, Cathy," Byron said from her comfortable position on the couch. "He's worried sick about you."

"Ah, I know he is, but he's driving me crazy."

"Aw, he'll calm down in a little while. Just remember, you gave him one hell of a scare. He's only trying to make sure you don't overdo things, that's all."

"I'll overdo him if he doesn't leave me alone. I know he means well, and I love him for it, but it's constant, By. 'Are you all right, Cathy? Can I get you anything, Cathy? What are you doing standing up, Cathy?'" She laughed as she mimicked Sam's voice.

"Ah, Cathy, you're terrible."

She shrugged. "Maybe you're right, but he nearly had a seizure when I told him you were all visiting today. He wanted to ring you back and tell you not to come." She sat back and held both hands out, still not believing it herself.

"But he's only trying to protect you," Bryon said. "You both had a big shock."

Cathy laughed. "I had to sit on the phone and warn him if he didn't start giving me an inch, I was going to kill him."

"He's worried. It's understandable."

"Ah, I know he is, and like I said, I love him for it, but I can't live between the couch and the bedroom for the next seven and a half months. I'm absolutely fine, By. Even the doctors said so. It was unfortunate that the baby decided to implant itself so close to a polyp, but now that it's gone, the baby and placenta are intact, and the doctors believe there's no future risk to me or the baby. Everything should be plain sailing from here on in."

"Beep, beep," Annabel said, coming back into the room, carrying a tray with mugs of fresh tea and slices of chocolate cake on plates."

Cathy groaned. "This is ridiculous. I could've made the tea." She got up to help.

"Sit down and shut up." Annabel pointed at the couch, then handed her a mug of steaming tea.

"Come on, Annabel," Byron said, "Finish your story."

"Oh, yes." She swallowed down a mouthful of cake, licking the residue off her lips. "Well, apparently, Jean Luc met Gemma last summer. They went out a few times, dinner and drinks, but never slept together. He said she was fine on the first couple of dates, but by the third or fourth meeting, she was acting possessive and needy, so he decided to cut her free."

"Too right," Byron said, "and it's a good job he did, by the sound of it."

Annabel nodded her agreement. "I know. He said he tried to cut all contact, but she continued to text and leave voice messages, refusing to believe their dates were nothing more than causal. She basically didn't want to let him go."

"He never slept with her?" Cathy asked. "How did she not get the message?"

"Sounds to me like she wasn't listening hard enough?" Byron said.

Annabel picked up another piece of cake. "Anyway, not long after, Jean Luc met me and you both know how we hit it off straight away."

"Yes, you did, you dirty stop-out," Cathy said, grinning from ear to ear. "I remember at that charity gala dinner, the two of you couldn't keep your hands off each other."

Byron choked on her tea. "You're one to talk, Cathy Byrne. As far as I remember, you and Sam disappeared into the hotel's disabled bathroom for a quick *how's-your-father*, right after the meal."

Cathy had forgotten she'd shared that piece of information. Her face burnt at the thought of it. "But we're not talking about me, are we? It's Annabel and Jean Luc who are the centre of this story, so leave me and Sam out of it."

"Anyway," Annabel said, gesturing for some order, "Jean Luc says that Gemma was still ringing and texting, even after we started dating. He went home one evening to find her camped out on his doorstep, in floods of tears."

"What was wrong with her now?" Byron asked, her deep scowl showing her annoyance.

"She wanted to know why she'd seen Jean Luc out in town with another woman." Annabel pointed at herself. "Me."

"Jesus." Byron shook her head and groaned. "This one has a screw lose."

"Jean Luc gave her short shrift that night. Told her to leave him alone, even threatened her with legal action if she ever came near him or his house again. A couple of weeks later, a package arrived at his house. It contained a single red rose, the petals crushed and torn, the stem broken and sellotaped in the middle, with all the thorns pulled off and scattered around the box. There was also a lock of blond hair, tied with a ribbon, lying beside the rose, and a photograph of Gemma, stark naked, with the rose pressed between her breasts, blood running from where the thorns had punctured her skin."

The room was silent. Nobody moved a muscle for several seconds. Cathy didn't know what to say about such a disturbing image. The girl was obviously mentally unstable and now had a bone to pick with one of them. With her friend.

Byron shook her head, the action a quick flick, as if trying to dislodge the image from her mind. "So how did she start working at your place?"

"I honestly don't know," Annabel answered. "She joined the company about eight or nine weeks ago. I don't suppose it would be difficult to find out where someone works, if you ask the right people. I'm fairly out there on the social scene, so it was just a matter of her finding the company and getting herself hired. If she couldn't get to Jean Luc directly, it looks like she's planning to go through me."

Cathy closed her eyes as a thought struck her. "Please tell me you're not going to work tomorrow, Annabel. You never know when the crazy bitch will snap and lash out at you. In fact, you're lucky she hasn't already."

"I was thinking that, too," Annabel admitted, "but don't worry, I'm owed time off so I emailed my boss this morning, letting her know I wouldn't be in for the next few days."

"Good plan," Byron said. "But what about Gemma?"

"Jean Luc is waiting for the detective he was dealing with about the picture and the rose to call him back, which will probably be tomorrow. He's going to get a restraining order for both of us against her. I have to admit, it's a little strange that he still has a copy of the picture on his phone, but he doesn't want the only copy to be held as Garda evidence, in case it gets lost or destroyed."

"That's good thinking," Cathy said. "It's the only evidence either of you have against her for now. Better to be safe than sorry."

Annabel held a fist up. "I'd love to thump the bitch, but I know it's best to leave it to the professionals. They'll get the evidence against her and bring her down a peg or two."

Byron twirled a finger at her temple. "Well, I've come across a lot of weirdos in my time, but that nut job is a paid up member of the bunny-boiler club."

Cathy didn't like where this was all going. "Annabel, you need to be careful. Keep out of her way. Don't be afraid to go to the Gardai if this escalates. This Gemma one sounds dangerous."

"Yeah, I know," Annabel said, "I was a bit freaked out last night when Jean Luc told me the full story and I realised how close she'd gotten to me. I wish she could be fired from work, but I've no evidence that she's done anything to me there, so hopefully the restraining order will give her the fright she needs to leave me alone."

Cathy reached over and took her hand. "Just promise us you'll be careful and tell us if there's any way we can help."

"Well, she'd better not meet me in a dark alley at night," Byron said, standing up and punching her fist into her other hand. "Nobody messes with me or my girls, not now, not ever, right?"

"Right," they agreed, especially Annabel.

28th April

Monday

Gary brought the children to school, as arranged with Cathy. Unable to stop himself, he drove the short distance from the school gates back to her house. Even when he spotted Sam's fancy car parked outside, he didn't falter – his need to see that his ex-wife was okay was too strong.

When he'd collected the children on Saturday, Cathy had been asleep in bed, and he'd worried all weekend. He didn't know exactly what had happened to her, he just hoped his advances towards her last week hadn't been the cause. All he knew was that she'd been extremely unwell, but now was home and the baby was still alive.

Sam answered the door. "What are you doing here?" He stood taller, filling the doorway with his whole body.

"Hi, Sam. Look, I don't want any trouble." He noticed the guy's puffed-out chest and remembered their last one-on-one encounter, which he'd not come out of well. "I just wanted to see if Cathy's all right. I was speaking with her mother on Saturday when I collected Millie and Jack, but I wanted to see how she was doing for myself." He waited, looking anywhere but at Sam's eyes.

Sam nearly growled as he stood back to let Gary enter, gesturing for him to go into the kitchen.

Cathy was having breakfast. Dressed in navy tracksuit pants and a bright pink t-shirt, she didn't look sick. Her cheeks were rosy, and he couldn't help catching her tell-tale lavender scent. He remembered her love for long, aromatic baths. It might have been the light coming in the kitchen window, he didn't know, but her skin glowed in a way he hadn't seen in ages.

She looked up. "Gary? What are you doing here?"

"Is this a double act?" he asked, a nervous laugh escaping. "That's exactly what I got at the door." He nodded at Sam. No one else laughed, but Sam edged closer behind him.

"Well?" Cathy's forehead creased as she waited for his answer.

"Ah, I heard you weren't well." He shuffled from foot to foot, only too aware of Sam's presence. "I, eh…heard you had a bit of a scare the other day."

"Sit down," she said, gesturing to the chair opposite her. "Would you like a cup of tea?"

He looked from her to Sam. The big oaf still standing there, like he was a bouncer. "Eh, okay, sure." He sat at the table he'd helped pick out when they'd first moved into this house. *My house.* Sam walked across the kitchen and lifted the kettle, but Cathy stood.

"I'll do it, Sam." She placed a hand on his arm. Gary caught her brief eye-flick before Sam retreated over to the sink.

"I'm sorry that happened to you," Gary said. "Is everything okay now?" He gestured in the general direction of her stomach.

"Everything is grand, and yes, I'm still pregnant, if that's what you're asking?"

"No, no, I wasn't asking that. Jesus." He rubbed his face. "I just hope none of this had anything to do with me?"

"What?" She stared at him. Sam stepped away from the sink.

"Well, you know, sometimes these things are brought on by stress, and after what I said to you last week, I just—"

"What did you say to her last week?" Sam asked, his voice low and dangerous as he stepped closer.

Cathy waved him away. "Please, Sam, I'll deal with this." She rubbed his shoulder and guided him back to the sink. Then she turned and glared at Gary. "It was a ruptured polyp, Gary. It would have happened even if I was lying on a beach soaking up the Caribbean sun. Nothing to do with stress...or anything else."

Gary breathed a sigh of relief at that. "Okay, because I was a bit concerned. The children have been great all weekend – good as gold, but they were worried about you, too. I wanted to see for myself that you were okay."

"What did you say to Cathy last week?" Sam asked again, his narrowed eyes hinting at his desire to rip Gary's head off.

Gary swallowed hard at the bloke's blatant aggressiveness, but thought it interesting that Cathy hadn't told him what he'd said. He caught her pleading look and decided not to play it. "Ah, it was nothing. We were just reminiscing about the twins when they were babies, then Cathy told me she was pregnant. That's all."

Sam landed Cathy with a questioning look, one eyebrow raised.

"Yep, that was pretty much the gist of it," she said, her words cutting through the tension.

"Look, I should go." He got up to leave them in peace, confident enough that Sam wouldn't try anything in front of Cathy, but he didn't want to risk it. He'd had more than enough with the last beating. "I'm happy you're okay. If you need me to take the kids any extra days, just let me know. We can work something out. All right?"

Cathy followed him out to the front door, obviously having told the oaf to stay in the kitchen.

"Sorry, I shouldn't have mentioned what I said last week." He reached for the door handle. "Thanks for covering for me."

"I didn't cover for you, you twat. I felt sorry for you."

Gary just stared, shocked at her anger. "What?"

"It actually slipped my mind last week and I forgot to tell him. Sam and I don't have secrets from one another. I have more important things to be concerned about, Gary, and your declaration of love last week certainly isn't one of them." She glanced back at the kitchen before leaning closer. "But now that you've reminded me, I'll make a point of telling him."

She followed him as he walked to his car. "The only reason I didn't say it to him in there, is because I knew he'd kill you stone dead. It's better I tell him when you're gone. There'll be less blood."

Gary swallowed and got into the car, fumbling with his keys.

She held the door open. "The only thing you have to worry about is when Sam finally flips his lid and comes after you. Because, believe you me, whatever little stunt you tried to pull in there, winding Sam up like that, it's not going to work. He is so much stronger than you could ever hope to be."

Gary knew that saying anything would only make things worse. Better to leave now and let them all calm down. Sam would understand where he was coming from. He was a bloke, after all. The key finally fitted into its slot and he started the engine. He had to give up now and accept that she was gone.

Sam had won the ultimate prize and, no matter what, Cathy would never be coming back to him. He took a deep breath and just nodded, then closed the car door, pulled out slowly, and drove away, tears burning into the back of his eyes.

29th April

Tuesday

With the day off work, Annabel decided to walk the short distance into town to enjoy some window-shopping on Dublin's Grafton Street.

Jean Luc was at meetings all day but he'd reassured her this morning that everything would be fine. The Gardaí were dealing with Gemma after he'd spoke with the detective on the phone yesterday. She didn't actually hear the conversation, but he said they'd spoken with Gemma at some stage during the day, and she'd admitted to everything: the redirecting of funds, all the ridiculous lies she'd spread at work, as well as the photo with the rose. The Gardaí served her with a restraining order and warned her to keep well away from both of them. Hopefully that was the end of the matter, as far as they were concerned.

She walked briskly through St Stephens Green, heading for Grafton Street, enjoying the freshness of the morning and the new spring colours along the garden borders.

Someone grabbed her arm from behind, dragging her backwards and off the main path. *What the hell?* She couldn't believe this was happening to her. It was broad daylight, in the middle of a busy Dublin park, and she was being mugged?

Before she had time to scream for help, she was swung around, bringing her face to face with the last person she wanted to see. Gemma.

"What the hell are you doing?" She tried to shake the mad bitch off. "Let go of me!"

Gemma released her grip, but blocked Annabel's escape back onto the path. Annabel rubbed her arm and moved to push past her, panic clutching at her throat, stifling her ability to breathe, or scream. *What will this lunatic do next?*

She found the strength to move her legs, summoning all the courage she had to get past this woman and run for help. With fierce resolve, she pushed at her adversary. "Get out of my way!"

"You got me fired," Gemma said, pulling her back with surprising strength.

"What are you talking about? The Gardaí said they gave you a warning, explained the restraining orders against you. No one said anything about losing your job."

"Oh, really?" Gemma sneered, her eyes dark, even when she moved out of the shadows. "I don't suppose it has anything to do with the Gardaí marching into the office yesterday afternoon and taking me to the station for questioning? Do you think it was just a coincidence that this morning I was called into the HR manager's office and told that my contract was being terminated with immediate effect?"

Annabel couldn't believe this was happening. She looked around to see if she was being filmed by a reality TV show, almost convinced she was being set up.

"Gemma, I'm sorry you lost your job, but I don't think that has anything to do with me." Her legs shook and she felt less secure as the seconds passed. Lots of people were moving along the pathway just a few meters away, but they couldn't see through the surrounding hedges and shrubs. She didn't like being face to face with this woman, who was obviously unstable, and quite capable of causing real harm.

As she watched Gemma's eyes, she threaded her fingers over her phone in her jacket pocket, unlocking it using the fingerprint password. She would try to talk some sense into this woman before things went too far, but needed to be prepared to ring the Gardaí at a moment's notice.

"What do you want from me?" she asked. "You were told to stay well away from me and Jean Luc. You're breaking the restraining order. Why shouldn't I ring the Gardaí?"

A wicked smile spread across Gemma's face, her whole demeanour taking on a coquettish pose at the mention of Jean Luc's name. "Ah, yes, Jean Luc." Her eyebrows wiggled and her eyes lit up. "The one that got away."

Horrified, Annabel could only stare, waiting to see where this was going. *What the hell did she mean by that?*

"Did he ever get around to telling you how he was still sleeping with me when he started sleeping with you?" Gemma crossed her legs, both hands on hips, swivelling insanely while her eyes never left

Annabel's. "In fact, we were perfectly happy in each other's arms until just before he went away."

Annabel stumbled back, the shock of her words stabbing at her heart. She didn't believe one syllable coming out of Gemma's mouth, and there was no way it could be true. But having dealt with her before, she knew how convincing the woman could sound when she spoke about something you didn't want to hear.

She decided this was a good time to get the police involved. This whole thing was turning nasty very fast. "You're crazy, Gemma. You don't know what you're saying." She pulled out her phone. "I'm calling the Gardai."

Gemma laughed at her, then slapped her hand, knocking the phone to the ground before stomping on it.

"Let me talk," she said, shoving Annabel back until she fell on the grass. "Did Jean Luc not tell you about all the hot meetings we had on those nights when you were too busy playing with your friends. Who would tend to his needs?" She held her hands out and raised a questioning eyebrow. "It's okay, I was there to look after him."

She circled Annabel, as if preying on a trapped animal. Annabel sat, too terrified to move an inch.

"What about our lunchtime romps? Didn't he tell you about them? How we would satisfy each other in a little hotel room, then I would go back to work and sit beside you in a meeting, wearing his scent. But you never noticed, did you?"

Choked by disbelief and a strangling fear, Annabel couldn't speak, couldn't argue back, or ask the single question of how this could be true.

Gemma leaned down to her. "Where do you think Jean Luc spent his last night in Ireland before he flew to the Emirates?"

Annabel's brain jolted into gear. She remembered that night well. Jean Luc had taken her for an early dinner, then back to his apartment. After making love a number of times, they'd fallen asleep because he had an early flight the next morning.

They'd both woke up around midnight, when the management company of Annabel's residential complex phoned to say her house alarm had been activated and she needed to go home.

Her head snapped up to stare at Gemma. "You threw the brick at my front door, setting off the alarm?"

Gemma grinned, looking like the cat that got more than the cream. She licked her lips, slow and wet, making Annabel's stomach lurch.

"Jean Luc didn't go with you to your house that night, did he?"

"No," Annabel answered, shocked she was actually answering this woman, falling into her trap. "I told him to stay and get some sleep, that I would meet the management company at the house and get things sorted."

"He didn't go back to sleep, Annabel. He came over to stay with me. And he didn't have an early morning flight." She chuckled. "In fact, his flight wasn't until the following day. We spent twenty-four glorious hours rolling around in my bed, getting very hot and sweaty. Jean Luc wanted to spend every last minute with the real love of his life, before he left. Me!"

Annabel shuddered, the damp grass soaking through her jeans. But it wasn't just the cold she felt. Fear crept through her, tightening its grip on her heart and soul. *It just can't be true.* "This is all lies, Gemma. Lies!" It was all she could say to stand up for herself and her sanity.

"Do you really think so?" The other woman remained buoyant, and Annabel realised she had more cards to play. "Do you really think I'm desperate enough to make all this up?"

"Yes, Gemma!" she spat back, finding the strength to lift her voice and let the nutcase have it with both barrels. "You're making it all up, because you're a mad, crazy bitch, living out a fantasy in your own warped little world. Why would Jean Luc go anywhere near someone like you? This is all bullshit. Now let me fucking go before I use you for a shortcut out of here." She stood up, wiped leaves and mud off her clothes, not willing to give this mad cow one more second of her time. She grabbed her smashed phone up and picked her path back off the grass verge, putting distance between them. Tears stung her eyes, but she was dammed if she would let them fall while Gemma was still there. She heard the other woman call to her.

"If this is all such bullshit, Annabel, why don't you ask yourself a very important question?"

Annabel turned, tensing herself as she faced this insane woman. "And what question is that?"

Gemma held her poise, a smirk lifting the corner of her mouth, as if confident her coming words would hit the mark. "If this is all bullshit, Annabel, why does Jean Luc still have naked pictures of me on his phone?"

30th April

Wednesday

Annabel had to drag herself awake. Her eyes were sore from lack of sleep and way too much crying. Looking around, she drew comfort from the familiar surroundings of her childhood bedroom. Framed awards from school and university hung on the walls, peppered with photographs of holidays and friends in between. The neat dressing table by the window still held old bottles of cheap perfumes: White Musk from the Body Shop and a bottle of CK One, the two staple fragrances of any young girl growing up in Ireland in the early Noughties.

Plush stuffed animals and bears rested on every available surface, keeping a watchful eye over her now, but also holding memories and secrets of everything they'd already seen in the years gone by: first crushes, first kiss, first heartbreak; it had all taken place in this room. If only those stuffed bears could talk. She hugged her favourite one close.

"What do you think, Mr Bumble?" she whispered in the old Steiff bear's ear. "Is this the most foolish I've ever been?"

Mr Bumble remained silent, but continued to provide warmth and comfort as she held him to her chest.

Now fully awake and deciding that sleep was futile, she got up and made her way downstairs. The old cooking range had kept the kitchen warm throughout the night, making the room welcoming at the early hour of a quarter-past-six.

Two hours' sleep. I can't go on like this. She brought her tea to the kitchen table by the window and looked out on the quiet spring morning. The rest of the world was waking up to a beautiful day, while she was stuck her in a bloody nightmare. She shook her head. How had she missed the signs? How had she gotten it so wrong? Was her infatuation with Jean Luc so strong that it prevented her from seeing what was going on right in front of her? No matter how many times she spun Gemma's words over in her mind, she just couldn't believe Jean Luc had done that to her. All the trouble she'd had at work was, it now seemed, just the tip of the iceberg. Gemma wasn't being spiteful or nasty to her because she wanted her job. She was weaving a bigger web of deceit because she wanted her man. Jean Luc was the prize, and it looked like the bitch had won.

Her stomach knotted as she remembered Gemma's final words to her. *"Why does Jean Luc still have naked pictures of me on his phone?"*

Again and again, she'd gone over the past six months in her mind. Every minute detail now faced deep analysis to see if the other girl could be telling the truth. Could Jean Luc have been declaring undying love to her while having an affair with another woman? Did he really do that to her?

It was too much to handle – the very thought of it making her sick. How could the man she loved, who she believed loved her back, be so cruel and uncaring?

"I'm a good person," she said to the empty room, choking on the emotion bubbling up from her chest. "Why did this happen to me?"

She sat for a while longer, contemplating the best plan of action, then got up to search for her new phone. At least she'd had the clear-headedness to save her SIM card. Her mother had wisely confiscated the phone last night, after Cathy and Byron had finished their group call. Cathy mentioned that Jean Luc had called her, begging her to hear him out, to tell him where Annabel was staying. It was all lies, he'd said, but of course, it was her word against his. Cathy told her how he'd tried desperately to convince her of his innocence in all of this, and that he was worried for Annabel's safety while he was no longer around to watch out for her. "We will look after her," Cathy had told him. "Annabel is our friend. Unlike you, we would never drag her through the shit and muck like you just have."

Her friends. Where would she be without them? Where would they be without each other? But she needed to be alone now, and she was safe here in her mother's house. Jean Luc had no idea where her childhood home was, so she wouldn't have to face him. She would choose when and where to speak to him – when the time was right for her.

The phone was behind the clock on the mantelpiece. As expected, there were a number of missed calls from Jean Luc. He'd been ringing nonstop since Annabel had yelled hysterically down the phone at him yesterday, telling him it was over and that Gemma was welcome to him. "The two of you will make a lovely couple," she'd screamed, before throwing the phone across the room.

Now, in the cold light of day, exhausted from crying and lack of sleep, she looked at the list of missed calls. The last one was at four a.m. He'd tried to contact her all night. She was glad her mother had taken the phone and muted it, because she knew her resolve wouldn't have held, and she would definitely have answered at some stage.

In a couple of days, she'd meet with Cathy and Byron. She needed them. It was their job to sit down and help her analyse everything that had happened, but for now all she wanted was to stay here, in this cosy house, and let her mother provide the comfort she desperately required.

***

Cathy and Byron spoke on the phone. Both were in shock about what had happened between Annabel and Gemma, and at how deceitful Jean Luc had turned out to be.

"I didn't see that coming, By, did you?"

"Not for a second. Sure he was only out with us all last weekend at your house. He seemed to be totally smitten with her. The shite never stopped touching her or smiling at her all day. What the fuck was this guy playing at?"

"I don't know," Cathy said, feeling so sorry for her friend. Annabel didn't deserve to be treated like that. No one did, but especially not her friend. "I'll tell you what, though, he sounded fairly convincing to me on the phone, when he rang to see if Annabel was staying here. He had me feeling a bit sorry for him by the end, if I'm honest."

"What, are you serious? Why else would Gemma go all mental over him? I know he's kind of hot, and French, and has an accent to die for, but do you actually think she was making it all up? Trying to break up Annabel's relationship with him just because she thinks they had something?"

"I don't know, By. But if this whole thing turns out to be true, he's one hell of an Oscar-winning actor, because he's sure as hell able to spin a story and work it his own way. But look," she continued, "the main thing is that we're there for her when she needs us to help pick up the pieces. We'll be there, however this mess plays out."

"I just can't believe it, Cathy. I swear, I'll do time if I ever get my hands on them. Her for being the scheming little bitch who's made Annie's life miserable for the past few months, and that other gobshite for putting her in so much danger. I could kill the two of them for what they've done to her."

"I agree," Cathy said, "because as far as I can make out, both of them have a screw loose."

"Her mam will look after her for the moment. We'll take on the next stage of the relationship-mourning. Whenever she's ready to curse and swear to high heaven, we'll be there to help her get it all out."

"Exactly," Cathy agreed. "We'll look after her. After all, what would any of us do without one another?"

"I know," Byron said, her voice quiet. "Even though you have the children and Sam, with this new baby on the way, and I'll be marrying the love of my life in six weeks, we always need our best friends to lean on, right?"

"In good times and in bad." Cathy knew they'd bring Annabel through this storm. They'd weathered many before, and no doubt there would be others in the future. It was who they were, true friends, always there for each other.

THE END

Thank you for reading this book, my second finished novel. I am completely overwhelmed with all the support and love shown to me after my first book, 30 days hath September was released. The incredible outpouring of love for Cathy and Sam was genuinely shocking for me. These two characters have lived in my head for many years, and for others to show an interest in what I was daydreaming about was flattering. The many text messages, Facebook, Twitter, Instagram posts, cards and emails I received, hollering at me for the next instalment, gave me the courage and strength to keep writing. I am thrilled to be able to let you take another peek inside my imagination, and hopefully help you fall in love with these friends and lovers, all over again.

See you all soon, for "June..."

Amy x

p.s. Thank you Sally, Natasha and AnneMarie. x

Book 1 in the Calendar Days Series is available to order from Amazon.co.uk as a paperback and download to your Kindle device or Kindle App.

30 days hath September

Amy Tierney

Turn the page to read an excerpt from 30 days hath September.

1st September 2013

SUNDAY

Cathy woke with her tongue stuck to the roof of her mouth, a cold wet hangover pounding at her temples.

"Thank God it's Sunday," she said, groaning as she rolled over to check the time. 11.45am the clock blinked. *Damn*, she would have to get up soon to collect the kids. They were starting back at school the next day and she still had pencil cases and new lunchboxes to buy. She knew this task could take all day if she wasn't careful. Depending on the availability of school accessories in the first shop they went to, she could end up having to spend the whole day in Dundrum Shopping Centre.

Once she managed to struggle out of bed, she headed for the shower, where she let the hot-water jets wash the night off her face and massage her shoulders, working her thick blonde hair into a shampoo lather. For Cathy, her morning shower was like the universe's way of giving her a fresh start; a blank canvas, to create on it whatever she chose. Some days she crafted beautiful masterpieces, akin to Michelangelo's work in the Sistine chapel. Sometimes she created crap, splashes of colour pulled together in no specific rhyme or reason, but mostly, she formed a nice simple pencil drawing detailing the easy, carefree attitude to life she'd begun to lead.

For a while, after she'd kicked Gary to touch, her canvases were black and grey, with a few spots of childish colour. It had been so hard dealing with her husband's betrayal, his cheating, forceful manner, and all the lying. The list went on and on like a bad song, scratching at her memory. While the first few weeks had passed in a daze of negative emotions, she'd eventually realised she could do one of two things: continue to paint a dull lifeless canvas for the rest of her days, or get out, cop on, and start living her life again. There was no option but to choose the latter. She had two children who were just as hurt and confused about the sudden change in their cosy family life. It broke her heart trying to comfort them while she also cursed Gary to hell for what he had done. It was clear to see that Jack and Millie were hurt enough without having to watch their mother wallow in a black hole.

One morning, after dropping the children to school, Cathy drove to the Black Castle beach, pent up and needing to find peace. With it being mid-November and still early, the small pebble bay lay deserted. As she breathed in the salty air, the ocean's energy caught her heart, its magnetic surge pulling her closer to the crashing waves. She dug her feet into the pebbles, took the deepest breath, and let it out in a long agonising scream. Not just once, but again, and again, screaming while hot tears rolled down her face, her hands clenched by her side, roaring into the wind, willing it to take her pain away, continuing until her eyes stung and her throat turned raw. Then she screamed a bit more, just for good measure.

Standing at the edge of the grey sea, she vowed to the seagulls circling above that she was done with the dark. These would be the last tears she would shed over that bastard. She banished her demons to the wind, forgiving her child within for all the rotten things she had thought about herself; for trying to understand and excuse why Gary had treated her so badly.

"It's over," she yelled at the seagulls. They duly obliged by swooping down to collect her sorrow and take it away. That chapter of her life was written and she was choosing to close the book. From now on, it was her and her children; Cathy's hopes and Cathy's dreams; her worries and sorrows, strengths and weaknesses. She had positives and negatives, rights and wrongs, for her to do with whatever she wanted. Right there, that morning, she started running, for herself.

***

Having dressed as fast as she could after her shower, she pulled her damp hair into a loose knot on top of her head. Once she'd applied mascara, she slid pale lip-gloss across her full lips, pouting into the bedroom mirror, telling herself she would have to do.

When she grabbed her jacket off the chair, she realised it still smelled from last night.

Being a Sunday afternoon, the traffic was light, and she enjoyed the sunny drive into Dublin to collect the children from the pub where Gary worked as a bar manager. Usually she didn't like the children being in a pub, but this was a family-run establishment and at this time on a Sunday would be full of parents with their kids enjoying a bit of pub grub for lunch.

After finding a space in the back car park, she made her way into the lounge, bubbling at the prospect of seeing her children. Gary, she could do without, but she missed Millie & Jack so much when they were with their dad. Even though Millie's constant yapping, and the inevitable arguments between the twins, drove her crazy, she suffered a terrible loneliness without them. After all, she had looked after them every day since they were born, nearly 6 years ago, and it came as no surprise that she still found it hard to deal with their absence, both when they went to school and to stay with their dad.

Making her way through the lounge, she spotted the twins sitting together on one side of a corner booth, Gary opposite them, looking confused. The children were eating lunch, which she was grateful to see. From the look of it, Gary had ordered a roast-beef dinner, and as she neared the table, the delicious aroma hit her. Scooting in beside the children, she gathered them into a bear hug and kissed the tops of their heads. Millie and Jack bounced beside her on the seat.

"Mammy! You're here," said Millie. "We are just having our lunch and telling Daddy about how it's okay for people to have two houses and two homes. Not everyone in our class has two houses, but some do, and that's okay. Right?"

Cathy glanced at Gary. Where had this come from? "Yep, it sure is," she said and gave Jack a quick wink. "Your lunch looks delicious, so be good and eat it all up before we go." Without thinking, she went into mammy mode by cutting their chicken nuggets a little smaller on each plate, making it easier for them to eat. She looked across at Gary.

"Hi, Cathy. How's things?"

She didn't want to get into any sort of conversation with Gary, but realised she had two sets of eyes watching her, so she made an effort to be civil.

"Great, not bad at all. That carvery looks nice." She nodded at his half-eaten dinner, then embarrassed herself with a loud grumble from her still-empty stomach, cursing her treacherous body. She agreed, at his suggestion, that she have some lunch before leaving. Usually, she would do anything to avoid spending even an extra second in her ex-husband's company, but today she was hungover, due her period, and in need of stodgy food to fill her up. Gary went to the bar to order her food, and returned with a jug of ice-cold water and a clean glass.

"Here, you look like you could use some of this."

He filled the glass and slid it across the table to her, always the professional barman, always ready to satisfy his customers' needs. Thing was, he'd never stopped at satisfying their drinking needs, taking it upon himself to look after their sexual requirements too.

A lounge boy came over with the food. As she looked up to pay him, she noticed a guy staring at her from behind the bar. The man focused on her with an intense, smouldering look. She squirmed before tearing her eyes away. Who is this hot guy checking her out in such an obvious way? She glanced at Gary, then looked back over to the bar and took in all that she could.

Tall, dark, and handsome. What a cliché. But that's what he was, his dark brown hair curling over the collar of his pristine-white shirt. Even at a distance, she made out the chocolate colour of his eyes, framed by long black lashes. He looked fit, too; strong, and oh-so-yummy.

He leaned forward as he spoke to a customer, but continued to look back to where Cathy sat. She tore her eyes away when he grinned at her, embarrassed to have been caught staring. Now, squirming in her seat, heat flushed into her face, and a knot tightened in the pit of her stomach.

"Who's the tall guy behind the bar?" she asked Gary, casual as could be.

"Sam?" He looked over. "He's been here a while."

"I don't recognise him." How could she have missed him before? "I thought I knew all the staff here?"

Gary smirked. "Oh, he's not staff, he's the boss."

"What?" She looked over to the bar to see if they were talking about the same person. "He couldn't be the boss. He's too young." And hot.

Gary filled her in on the mystery man.

"He's Sam O'Keefe, son of Michael O'Keefe. Part of the O'Keefe Empire and all who sails in her. They own this place and a few more around town. Pubs and Clubs. That's their tipple and it's done them well over the years."

"But how come I've never seen him before? Has he just been released from prison or something?" Maybe he'd been put away for crimes against passion. Jesus, where was this coming from? She flushed again at the thought.

She sensed that Gary wasn't happy with her new interest in Sam O'Keefe, but he answered her anyway.

"He just came back from abroad. Ibiza, I think, and the Balearic islands. As far as I know, he's been there for a few years. Now he's taken on the area-manager's job for the pub chain. This and two clubs on Leeson Street are part of his patch."

Cathy finished eating, checking that the children had enough and were happy with the colouring book Gary had brought. She looked back over to the bar, catching a glimpse of Sam as he disappeared into the back room. I shouldn't be checking him out. He's my ex-husband's boss. The ex-husband I'm sitting here with, having lunch with for the first time since we split. The ex-husband who I'm having the longest conversation with in a year, and it's about another man. A sexy man. A man whose eyes, even from here, melted into her. A man whose body looked like he could hold up to a marathon session in the bedroom. And a man who really was out of her league.

If Gary was right about Sam's family and pedigree, Cathy imagined he had women falling at his feet, throwing themselves at him, and generally had the pick of the bunch. No, she wasn't interested in heartbreak, but it was still nice to appreciate the dessert menu, even if you are on a diet. Sam O'Keefe was dessert for sure. The chocolate kind.

Dragging her thoughts out of the gutter, she told Gary that she'd enrolled the twins in a local after-school drama and dance class. It would help build

Jack's confidence and social skills, and Millie would be right at home having a stage to perform on.

"Sounds good," he said. "When does it start?"

She hated having to ask him for money, but when it was for the kids, it made it easier.

"That's the thing, it starts next week. I'm a bit short for the term fees, and was wondering if you could help out at all?"

"Of course, no problem." He said this as if money was never an issue for him, which it didn't seem to be. Gary earned a good wage, and always looked after them when they had been a family. Since the split, he still paid the mortgage and deposited a set amount into Cathy's account each month for the kids. It wasn't a fortune, and sometimes things were tight, but she managed. During the summer months, she took in ironing from a local B&B, and this gave her a few extra Euro to enjoy a bit of breathing space. She rarely had much left at the end of any week for the usual niceties, but she did her best to make sure the children didn't go without.

"It's just with the kids going back to school this week, it's a bit tight. You know, two of everything, and that includes term fees for any extra activities."

It annoyed her that she needed to justify to herself how she used the money Gary gave her. She didn't flit it away on nights out with the girls, or pampering weekends away when Gary had the kids. If he had noticed that she was taking better care of herself, he hadn't said anything. No, the money was spent on essentials like food, clothes, bills, except for the odd bottle of wine which she opened on a Friday and made last 'til Sunday. In fact, last night's drinks were a result of her friends Byron and Annabel dragging her out, plying her with cocktails to celebrate her surviving the past year, and coming out the other side of the wringer in one piece.

"It's not a problem, Cathy," Gary said, pulling her back to the moment. "How much do you need?"

She told him how much half the fees would be.

"I'll have it for you by the end of the week." He looked at this watch, then glanced up at the clock over the bar. "My shift will be starting soon."

"Right. Thing is, Gary, I'll need it by Wednesday at the latest. They start their first class after school and I need to have it paid by then. I appreciate the help-out. It takes the pressure off." She didn't miss that he failed to offer her any extra money, even though he knew she was struggling.

She leaned on the table so he would hear her over the general pub noise. "The drama and dance school will be great for them. They need to start mixing with other kids outside school. You know how dependent they are on each other. They even have the same friends in their class."

After the breakup, the children had clung to each other for comfort and familiarity in their changing world. Amazing as children are, they adjusted to their new family situation a lot quicker than Cathy had, but she still worried. They were so close, she dreaded the day when extravert Millie woke up interested in boys, with Jack, being the quieter of the two, getting left behind.

That was a few years away yet, but she didn't want them getting into any habits now that might hinder either of them in the future. They loved each other. They would always be each other's twin, but they were also individuals and they needed to be treated as such.

When the lounge boy returned to clear the table, Cathy gathered Millie and Jack up to leave.

"I'll walk you out to the car," Gary offered. He went over to the bar and returned with the twins' overnight bag. Cathy noticed Sam leave the office and make his way over to where they stood.

"Hi, Gary. Sorry to intrude. Are you on today?" Sam glanced at Cathy and the children.

"Yes, yes," Gary said, annoyance obvious in his response. "I'm just finishing up here. I'll be around to help in a minute."

Sam didn't make any move to leave so Gary took a deep breath and gestured between them with both hands. "Sorry, yeah, Sam, this is Cathy. Cathy, Sam O'Keefe."

Sam reached out and shook Cathy's hand with a firm grip. Not sure if Gary could see the spark that flew, she shook Sam's hand once then withdrew.

"Hi, guys," he said to Millie and Jack.

Cathy rubbed her hand on her thigh, noting how he was already familiar with her children.

"Thanks for the crisps yesterday, Sam," Millie said, grinning up at him. "They were yummy."

Sam smiled back. "Anytime, little lady." He leaned to his left. "How's your knee today, Jack? Is it better?"

Jack gave Sam a thumbs up as Cathy threw a sharp glare at Gary. She bent to inspect Jack's knees.

"I fell yesterday, Mammy," Jack said, a serious expression on his tiny upturned face, "and my knee was bleeding the red stuff. Sam got me a blue plaster from the kitchen and it fixed my broken leg."

"Good stuff, little man." Sam ruffled Jack's hair, winking at him. Millie giggled with delight at her new friend.

Cathy took it all in. How much time did the children spent here with their dad? It was obvious that they were used to Sam. She vowed to tackle Gary on the issue another time.

"We better get going," she said, eager to get away from this man who was sending shivers down her spine, and away from this other man who she wanted to kill with her bare hands for being so irresponsible with her children.

"Nice to meet you, Cathy," Sam said as she stepped away from the table.

Not wanting to be rude, Cathy paused, but then turned, catching her breath as her cheeks flushed. How is this guy having such an effect on me? She tightened her stomach muscles. "Nice to meet you, too, Sam. Enjoy the rest of your day." She didn't give him a chance to respond, walking with the twins out of the pub and into fresh air.

As she headed for the car, the children and Gary in tow, her blood boiled. How many times had Gary brought the kids here? She'd only collected them from here on a couple of occasions. It seemed, thought, they were here more than she knew. Enough that they knew the bar staff. And the bar staff knew them – even the new, hot, sexy, area manager, whose touch Cathy was trying hard to forget.

Strapping the kids into their car seats, she told Gary to call her about his days off next week. They would need to work something out if he was taking them mid-week. With them being back at school, she needed to know if he was able for the early-morning school runs.

***

She drove the twins to Dundrum Shopping Centre, going first to Tesco's for lunchboxes and then Eason's for the pencil cases, striking it lucky in both, delighted that she'd accomplished her objectives without having to trawl through a dozen shops.

Once home, they all got into their fluffy pyjamas, pulled the curtains closed, and snuggled up on the sofa to watch a Disney DVD. Cathy didn't pay much attention to the film she'd already seen about seventeen times. Instead, she thought back to the man she'd met earlier. Sam O'Keefe. Every time she thought about him, her belly flipped. She couldn't get his face out of her mind. The way he'd looked at her. He was charming. Although, something told her he was also trouble, and with her usual stubborn revolve she decided to steer well clear of him. She couldn't get involved with a heartbreaker again. No, she wouldn't survive it. She took her phone from her pocket and googled his name. Yes, she knew it, trouble. It was all there in black and white. Big trouble.

2nd September

Monday

Eight weeks of summer holidays had given Cathy plenty of precious time with Millie and Jack. Any warm and sunny day, she'd dropped everything, packed a bag, and headed to the beach with the children. Calm hot days were a rarity in Ireland and when the rain disappeared for three days in a row, it felt like they were in the south of France. The last two weeks of August had been wet and unpredictable, though, so she'd tried to entertain them at home, but there was only so much she could do.

Now, their first day back at school was a welcome relief for all of them. By 9.05 that morning, Millie and Jack were safely settled in the Senior-Infant classroom, sharing a small wooden table and sitting on miniature chairs. Excited shouts of welcome had greeted the children as they reconnected with friends, and parents gave brief rundowns of the exotics of their summer break.

Miffed at first for being unable to moan about delayed flights and lost luggage this year, Cathy brightened up after a quick chat with a few of the adults, realising that not everyone had been able to get abroad. More and more people were struggling in the economic downturn. Plenty of other families, like her own, had battled their way through the Irish summer and lived it up on the Costa Del Courtown, or headed out West instead.

***

Cathy changed into three-quarter-length leggings when she got home. A sloppy-white t-shirt and running shoes completed the outfit. Bringing her I-Pod, she drove to the port road in Wicklow Town, parking near the Black Castle beach. She stretched and twisted as she warmed up, then set off running.

After her screaming session with the seagulls last year, she'd often started her run from here, from what she saw as her symbolic spot. Her objective was to run at least twice, if not three times a week. In the beginning she'd nearly killed herself by going too far, too fast. The need to run away from her old life drove her forward, pushing herself into a new one. Then, after a while, she found her rhythm and it no longer caused her physical pain; the cramps in her legs disappeared and the burning in her lungs subsided.

These days she ran because she enjoyed it, free and uninhibited. Perhaps she still used it as a stress release, but whatever the reason for her running, it was working, both in her body and mind. She'd lost a huge amount of baby weight, slimming to a body she was comfortable with. Her legs and calves were toned and sculpted, and her skin had a beautiful sun-kissed, red-cheeked glow from being out in the fresh air. The extra exercise helped with her sleep too, sliding into a coma for the best part of six hours each night, exhausted from being a busy mammy and running 5km on a regular basis.

Gone were the times where she tossed and turned, tormenting herself with the haves and what-ifs. Insomnia had darkened her canvas and brought her to a new low. Now, night times were for sleeping, allowing her body and brain to recharge. Running was the time for thinking, for pounding out any worries or niggles with the ever-solid beat of her feet.

Sam O'Keefe's face kept popping up during her run, easing her pounding to a soft thread as she imagined him. Indulging in her fantasy, she endeavoured to block out all the crazy stuff she'd read about him on Google, concentrating instead on the feelings she'd experienced when he'd looked at her, right into her soul. She visualised him coming on to her, wanting her, drawing her into his space. The spark that flew with an electrical jolt when their hands touched was not the result of carpet static, that's for sure.

I'd love to hear from you.. Follow me on Facebook at http://fb.me/amytierneyauthor, https://twitter.com/kauto12 and _Amy Tierney Author_ on Instagram for news on upcoming readings, events and new releases.

42450738R00158

Made in the USA
Middletown, DE
12 April 2017